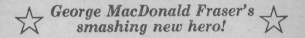

☆ *George MacDonald Fraser's* ☆
smashing new hero!

Meet Lt. Dand MacNeill ... staunch, shy, wry and really 100% unflappable ... a man in a million!

... and his merry band of kilted warriors on their hilarious odyssey homeward at the close of World War II ...

☆ Private McAuslan, the dirtiest soldier in the world
☆ Ahmed of the Thousand Fingers, who invented the Gaza Game
☆ The General who dreams of dancing a reel with 128 men
☆ The assorted Jocks, Arabs, Terrorists and Eccentrics rattling through Palestine on a troop train, suspected of German Measles

In a word, no wartime woes—but regimental humor in the grand old manner, spiced with affection for a world of camaraderie that is no more.

The General Danced at Dawn

and other stories

George MacDonald Fraser

BALLANTINE BOOKS • NEW YORK

"The General Danced at Dawn" and "Guard at the Castle" were first published in *Scotland's Magazine* under the by-line "By Dand MacNeill," and part of "Monsoon Selection Board" in *The Red Poppy*.

Library of Congress Catalog Card Number: 75-154923

SBN 345-24122-3-125

This edition published by arrangement with
Alfred A. Knopf, Inc.

First Printing: August, 1974

Cover art by Coconis

Printed in the United States of America

BALLANTINE BOOKS
A Division of Random House, Inc.
201 East 50th Street, New York, N.Y. 10022

For my father

AUTHOR'S NOTE

The Highland battalion in this book never existed, inasmuch as the people in the stories are fictitious (with the formidable exception of my grand-mothers), and the incidents have been made up from a wide variety of sources, including my imag-ination. As to traditions, customs, and one or two pieces of history, these too are a mixture, with one regimental strain predominating. But the atmo-sphere and background detail which I have tried to put into the book are as accurate as memory can make them.

G. M. F.

CONTENTS

Monsoon
Selection Board

OUR coal-bunker is old, and it stands beneath an ivy hedge, so that when I go to it in wet weather, I catch the combined smells of damp earth and decaying vegetation. And I can close my eyes and be thousands of miles away, up to my middle in a monsoon ditch in India, with my face pressed against the tall slats of a bamboo fence, and Martin-Duggan standing on my shoulders, swearing at me while the rain pelts down and soaks us. And all around there is mud, and mud, and more mud, until I quit dreaming and come back to the mundane business of getting a shovelful of coal for the sitting-room fire.

It is twenty years and more since I was in India. My battalion was down on the Sittang Bend, trying to stop the remnants of the Japanese Army escaping eastwards out of Burma — why we had to do this no one really understood, because the consensus of opinion was that the sooner Jap escaped the better, and good luck to him. Anyway, the war was nearly over, and one lance-corporal more or less on the battalion strength didn't make much difference, so they sent me out of the line to see if a War Office Selection Board would adjudge me fit to be commissioned.

I flew out and presented myself to the Board, bush-hat on head, beard on chin, kukri on hip, all in sweaty jungle green and as tough as a buttered muffin. Frankly, I had few hopes of being passed. I had been to a Board once before, back in England, and had fallen foul of a psychiatrist, a mean-looking little man who bit his nails and asked me if I had

an adventurous spirit. (War Office Selection Boards were always asking questions like that.) Of course, I told him I was
as adventurous as all get-out, and he helped himself to another piece of nail and said cunningly :

'Then why don't you sign on to sail on a Norwegian
whaler?'

This, in the middle of the war, mark you, to a conscript.
So, thinking he was being funny, I replied with equal cunning that I didn't speak Norwegian, ha-ha. He just loved
that; anyway, I didn't pass.

So I flew out of Burma without illusions. This particular
Board had a tough reputation; last time, the rumour went,
they had passed only three candidates out of thirty. I looked
round at my fellow applicants, most of whom had at least
three stripes and seemed to be full of confidence, initiative,
leadership, and flannel—qualities that Selection Boards lap up
like gravy — and decided that whoever was successful this
time it wasn't going to be me. There were two other Four-
teenth Army infantrymen, Martin-Duggan and Hayhurst,
and the three of us, being rabble, naturally drifted together.

I should explain about Selection Boards. They lasted
about three days, during which time the candidates were
put through a series of written and practical tests, and the
Board officers just watched and made notes. Then there
were interviews and discussions, and all the time you were
being assessed and graded, and at the finish you were told
whether you were in or out. If in, you went to an Officer
Cadet Training Unit where they trained you for six months
and then gave you your commission; if out, back to your
unit.

But the thing that was universally agreed was that there
was no known way of ensuring success before a Selection
Board. There were no standard right answers to their questions, because their methods were all supposed to be deeply
psychological. The general view throughout the Army was
that they weren't fit to select bus conductors, let alone
officers, but that is by the way.

One of the most unpleasant features of a Selection Board was that you were on test literally all the time. At meal times, for instance, there was an examining officer at each table of about six candidates, so we all drank our soup with exaggerated care, offered each other the salt with ponderous politeness, and talked on a plane so lofty that by comparison a conversation in the Athenaeum Club would have sounded like an argument in a gin-mill. And all the time our examiner, a smooth, beady gentleman, kept an eye on us and weighed us up while pretending to be a boon companion.

It wasn't too easy for him, for at our second meal I displayed such zeal in offering him a bottle of sauce that I put it in his lap. I saw my chances fading from that moment, and by the time we fell in outside for our first practical test my nerves were in rags.

It was one of those idiotic problems where six of you are given a log, representing a big gun-barrel, and have to get it across a river with the aid of a few ropes and poles. No one is put in command; you just have to cooperate, and the examiners hover around to see who displays most initiative, leadership, ingenuity, and what-have-you. The result is that everyone starts in at once telling the rest what to do. I had been there before, so I let them argue and tried to impress the Board by being practical. I cleverly tied a rope round the log, and barked a sharp command to Martin-Duggan and Hayhurst. They tugged on the rope and the whole damned thing went into the river. At this there was a deadly silence broken only by the audible scribbling of the examiners, and then the three of us sheepishly climbed down the bank to begin salvage operations.

This set the tone of our whole performance in the tests. Given a bell tent to erect we reduced it to a wreck of cord and canvas inside three minutes; ordered to carry from Point A to Point B an ammunition box which was too heavy for one man and which yet did not provide purchase for two, we dropped it in a ditch and unbraided each other in sulphurous terms, every word of which the examiners recorded carefully. Asked to swing across a small ravine on a rope, we betrayed symptoms of physical fear, and Hayhurst fell and hurt his ankle. Taking all in all, we showed ourselves lacking in initiative, deficient in moral fibre, prone to recrimination, and generally un-officer-like.

So it went on. We were interviewed by the psychiatrist, who asked Hayhurst whether he smoked. Hayhurst said no – he had actually given it up a few days before – and then noticed that the psychiatrist's eyes were fixed on his right index finger, which was still stained yellow with nicotine. My own interview was, I like to think, slightly less of a triumph from the psychiatrist's point of view. He asked me if I had an adventurous spirit, and I quickly said yes, so much so that my only regret about being in the Army was that it prevented me from signing on to sail on a Norwegian whaler.

If, at this point, he had said: 'Oh, do you speak Norwegian, then?' he would have had me over a barrel. But instead he fell back on the Selection Board classic, which is: 'Why do you want to be an officer?'

The honest answer, of course, is to say, like Israel Hands, 'Because I want their pickles and wines and that,' and to add that you are sick of being shoved around like low-life, and want to lord it over your fellow-man for a change. But honest answer never won fair psychiatrist yet, so I assumed my thoughtful, stuffed look, and said earnestly that I simply wanted to serve the Army in my most useful capacity, and I felt, honestly, sir, that I could do the job. The pay was a lot better, too, but I kept that thought to myself.

He pursed up and nodded, and then said: 'I see you want to be commissioned in the — Highlanders. They're a pretty tough bunch, you know. Think you can handle a platoon of them?'

I gave him my straight-between-the-eyes look which, coupled with my twisted smile, tells people that I'm a lobo wolf from Kelvinside and it's my night to howl. Just for good measure I added a confident, grating laugh, and he asked with sudden concern if I was going to be sick. I quickly reassured him, but he kept eyeing me askance and presently he dismissed me. As I went out he was scribbling like crazy.

Then there were written tests, in one of which we had to record our instant reactions to various words flashed on a blackboard. With me there was not one reaction in each case, but three. The first was just a mental numbness, the second was the reaction which I imagined the examiners would regard as normal and the third (which naturally was what I finished up writing down) was the reaction which I was sure would be regarded as abnormal to a degree. Some people are like this: they are compelled to touch naked electric wiring and throw themselves down from heights. Some perverse streak makes them seek out the wrong answers.

Thus, given the word 'board', I knew perfectly well that the safe answer would be 'plank' (unless you chose to think that 'board' meant 'Selection Board', in which case you would write down 'justice', 'mercy', or 'wisdom'). But with the death wish in full control I had to write down 'stiff'.

Similarly, reason told me to react to 'cloud', 'father', and 'sex' by writing down 'rain', 'W. G. Grace', and 'birds and bees'. So of course I put down 'cuckoo', 'Captain Hook', and 'Grable'. To make matters worse I then scored 'Grable' out in a panic and wrote 'Freud', and then changed my mind again, scoring out 'Freud' and substituting 'Lamour'. Heavy breathing at my elbow at this point attracted my attention, and there was one of the examiners, peeking at my paper with his eyes bulging. By this time I was falling behind in my reactions, and was in such a frenzied state that when they eventually flashed 'Freud' on the board I think my response was 'Father Grable'. That must have made them think.

They then showed us pictures, and we had to write a story about each one. The first picture showed a wretch, with an expression of petrified horror on his face, clinging to a rope. Well, that was fairly obviously a candidate escaping from a Selection Board and discovering that his flight was being observed by a team of examiners taking copious notes. Then there was a picture of a character with a face straight out of Edgar Allan Poe, being apprehended by a policeman. (Easy: the miscreant was the former principal of a Selection Board, cashiered for drunkenness and embezzlement, and forced to beg his bread in the gutter, being arrested for vagrancy by a copper who turned out to be a failed candidate.)

But the one that put years on all the many hundreds of candidates who must have regarded it with uninspired misery was of an angelic little boy sitting staring soulfully at a violin. There are men all over the world today who will remember that picture when Rembrandt's 'Night Watch' is forgotten. As art it was probably execrable, and as a mental stimulant it was the original lead balloon. Just the sight of that smug, curly-headed little Bubbles filled you with a sense of gloom. One Indian candidate was so affected by it that he began to weep; Hayhurst, after much mental anguish, produced the idea that it was one of Fagin's apprentices gloating over his first haul; my own thought was that the picture represented the infant Stradivarius coming to the conclusion that given a well-organized sweat-shop there was probably money in it.

Only Martin-Duggan dealt with the thing at length; the picture stirred something in his poetic Irish soul. The little boy, he recorded for the benefit of the examiners, was undoubtedly the son of a famous concert violinist. His daddy had been called up to the Forces during the war, and the little boy was left at home, gazing sadly at the violin which his father would have no opportunity of playing until the war was over. The little boy was terribly upset about this, the thought of his father's wonderful music being silenced; he felt sure his daddy would pine away through being deprived of his violin-playing. Let the little boy take heart, said Martin-Duggan; he needn't worry, because if his daddy played his cards right he would get himself promoted to the post of quartermaster, and then he would be able to fiddle as much as he liked.

Martin-Duggan was terribly pleased with this effort; the poor sap didn't seem to understand that in military circles a joke is only as funny as the rank of its author is exalted, and Martin-Duggan's rank couldn't have been lower.

Of course, by the time the written tests were over, the three of us were quite certain that we were done for. Our showing had probably been about as bad as it could be, we thought, and our approach to the final ordeal of the Selection Board, on the third afternoon, was casual, not to say resigned. This was a trip over the assault course – a military obstacle race in which you tear across country, climb walls, swing on ropes, crawl through tunnels, and jump off ramps. The climax is usually something pretty horrid, and in this case it consisted of a monsoon ditch four feet deep in water, at the end of which was a huge bamboo fence up which you had to climb in three-man teams, helping each other and showing initiative, intelligence, cheerfulness, and other officer-like qualities, if possible.

We were the last three over, and as we waded up the ditch, encouraging each other with military cries, the rain was lashing down something awful. There was a covered shelter overlooking the ditch, and it was crammed with examiners – all writing away as they observed the floundering candidates – as well as the top brass of the Board. All the other candidates had successfully scaled the fence, and were standing dripping with mud and water, waiting to see how we came on.

Our performance, viewed from the bank, must have been something to see. I stood up to my waist in water against the fence, and Martin-Duggan climbed on my shoulders, and Hayhurst climbed on his, and I collapsed, and we all went under. We did this about five or six times, and the gallery hooted with mirth. Martin-Duggan, who was a proud, sensitive soul, got mad, and swore at me and kicked me, and Hayhurst made a tremendous effort and got on to the top of the fence. He pulled Martin-Duggan up, and the pair of them tried to pull me up, too, but I wasn't having any. I was rooted up to my middle in the sludge, and there I was going to stay, although I made it look as though I was trying like hell to get up.

They tugged and strained and swore, and eventually Martin-Duggan slipped and came down with a monumental splash, and Hayhurst climbed down as well. The spectators by this time were in hysterics, and when we had made three or four more futile efforts — during which I never emerged from the water once — the officer commanding the Board leaned forward and said :

'Don't you chaps think you'd better call it a day?'

I don't know what Martin-Duggan, a mud-soaked spectre, was going to reply, but I beat him to it. Some Heaven-sent inspiration struck me, because I said, in the most soapy, sycophantic, Eric-or-Little-by-Little voice I have ever used in my life :

'Thank you, sir, we'd prefer to finish the course.'

It must have sounded impressive, for the CO stood back, almost humbly, and motioned us to continue. So we did, floundering on with tremendous zeal and getting nowhere, until we were almost too weary to stand and so mud-spattered that we were hardly recognizable as human beings. And the CO, bless him, leaned forward again, and I'll swear there was a catch in his voice as he said :

'Right, that's enough. Well tried. And even if you didn't finish it, there's one thing I'd like to say. I admire guts.' And all the examiners, writing for dear life, made muted murmurs of assent.

What they and the CO didn't know was that my trousers had come off while we were still wading up the ditch, and that was why I had never budged out of the water and why we had never got up the fence. A good deal I had endured, but I was not going to appear soaked and in my shirt-tail before all the Board and candidates, not for anything. And as we waded back down the ditch and out of sight round the bend, I told Martin-Duggan and Hayhurst so.

And we passed, I suppose because we showed grit, determination, endurance, and all the rest of it. Although with Selection Boards you never could tell. Only three of us know that what got us through was the loss of my pants, and military history has been made out of stranger things than that.

Silence in the Ranks

THE life of the very young officer is full of surprises, and perhaps the most shaking is the moment when he comes face to face with his men for the first time. His new sergeant stamps to a halt in front of him, salutes, and barks: 'Platoon-presnready-frinspeckshun-sah!', and as he clears his throat and regards the thirty still figures, each looking to its front with frozen intensity, the young subaltern realizes that this is it, at last; this is what he is drawing his meagre pay for.

In later years he may command armies or govern great territories, but he will never feel again the same power-drunk humility of the moment when he takes over his platoon. It is elating and terrifying – mostly terrifying. These thirty men are his responsibility, to look after, to supervise, to lead (whatever that means). Of course, they will do what he tells them – or he hopes they will, anyway. Suppose they don't? Suppose that ugly one in the front rank suddenly says 'No, I will not slope arms for you, or shave in the morning, or die for king and country'? The subaltern feels panic stealing over him, until he remembers that at his elbow there is a sergeant, who is wise in dealing with these matters, and he feels better.

There are young officers, of course, who seem to regard themselves as born to the job, and who cruise through their first platoon inspection with nonchalant interest, conversing airily with the sergeant as they go; possibly Hannibal and Napoleon were like that. But I doubt it. A man would have to be curiously insensitive not to realize that for the first time in his life thirty total strangers are regarding him with interest and suspicion and anxiety, wondering if he is a soft mark or a complete pig, or worse still, some kind of nut. When he realizes this he feels like telling them that he is, really, all right and on their side, but of course he can't. If he did, they would know for certain he was some kind of nut. They will just have to find out about each other gradually, and it can be a trying process.

I have only a hazy impression of inspecting my platoon for the first time. They were drawn up in the sunlight with their backs to the white barrack wall, against which an Arab tea-vendor was squatting, waiting for the ten-minute break. But all I can remember is the brown young faces staring earnestly to their front, with here and there a trickle of sweat or a limb shaking with the strain of standing still. I remember telling one that he was smartly turned-out, and he gave a controlled shudder, like a galvanized frog, and licked his lips nervously. I asked another whether he had volunteered for this particular regiment, and he stammered: 'Nossir, I wanted to go intae the coal-mines.'

Perhaps I was over-sensitive because I had been more than two years in the ranks myself, and had stood sweating while pinkish young men with one painfully new pip on their shoulders had looked at me. I remembered what I had thought about them, and how we had discussed them afterwards. We had noted their peculiarities, and now I wondered what mine were – what foibles and mannerisms were being observed and docketed, and what they would say about me later.

I don't know what I expected from that first inspection – a rapturous welcome, three cheers, or an outbreak of mutiny – but what I got was nothing at all. It was a bit damping; they didn't seem to react to me one way or the other. Maybe I should have made a speech, or at least said a few introductory words, but all that I could think of was Charles Laughton's address to the crew of the *Bounty*, which ran: 'You don't know wood from canvas, and you evidently don't want to learn. Well, I'll teach you.' It wouldn't have gone over.

So eventually I watched them fall out, and turn from wooden images into noisy, raucous young men crowding round the tea-man, abusing him happily in Glasgow-Arabic. One or two glanced in my direction, briefly, but that was all. I walked back to the company office, suddenly lonely.

The trouble was, of course, that in the exultation of being commissioned at the end of a hectic training in India, and the excitement of journeying through the Middle East and seeing the wonderful sights, and arriving in this new battalion which was to be home, I had overlooked the fact that all these things were secondary. What it all added up to was those thirty people and me; that was why the King had made me 'his trusty and well-beloved friend'. I wondered, not for the first time, if I was fit for it.

It had seemed to go well on the day of my arrival. The very sound of Scottish voices again, the air of friendly informality which you find in Highland regiments, the sound of pipe music, had all been reassuring. My initial discomfort – I had arrived with two other second lieutenants, and while they had been correctly dressed in khaki drill I had still been wearing the jungle green of the Far East, which obviously no one in the battalion had seen before – had quickly blown over. The mess was friendly, a mixture of local Scots accents and Sandhurst drawls, and my first apprehensions on meeting the Colonel had been unfounded. He was tall and bald and moustached, with a face like a vulture and a handkerchief tucked in his cuff, and he shook hands as though he was really glad to see me.

Next morning in his office, before dispatching me to a company, he gave me sound advice, much of which passed me by although I remembered it later.

"You've been in the ranks. Good. That' – and he pointed to my Burma ribbon – 'will be a help. Your Jocks will know you've been around, so you may be spared some of the more

elementary try-ons. I'm sending you to D Company – my
old company, by the way.' He puffed at his pipe thought-
full. 'Good company. Their march is *The Black Bear*, which
is dam' difficult to march to, actually, but good fun. There's
a bit where the Jocks always stamp, one-two, and give a
great yell. However, that's by the way. What I want to tell
you is : get to know their names; that's essential, of course.
After a bit you'll get to know the nicknames, too, probably,
including your own. But once you know their names and
faces, you'll be all right.'

He hummed on a bit, and I nodded obediently and then
took myself across to D Company office, where the company
commander, a tall, blond-moustached Old Etonian named
Bennet-Bruce, fell on me with enthusiasm. Plainly D Company, and indeed the entire battalion, had just been waiting
a couple of centuries for this moment; Bennet-Bruce was
blessed above all other company commanders in that he
had got the new subaltern.

'Splendid. Absolutely super. First-class.' He pumped me
by the hand and shouted for the Company clerk. 'Cormack,
could you find another cup for Mr MacNeill? This is Cormack, invaluable chap, has some illicit agreement with the
Naafi manager about tea and excellent pink cakes. Mr Mac-
Neill, who has joined our company. You do take sugar?
First class, good show.'

I had been in the Army quite long enough not to mistake
Bennet-Bruce for just a genial, carefree head-case, or to
think that because he prattled inconsequentially he was
therefore soft. I'd seen these caricature types before, and
nine times out of ten there was a pretty hard man underneath. This one had the *Médaille Militaire*, I noticed, and
the French don't hand that out for nothing.

However, he was making me at home, and presently he
wafted me round the Company offices and barrack-rooms
on a wave of running commentary.

'Company stores here, presided over by Quarter-master
Cameron, otherwise known as Blind Sixty. Biggest rogue in

the Army, of course, but a first-class man. First-class. Magazine over there – that's Private Macpherson, by the way, who refuses to wear socks. Why won't you wear socks, Macpherson?'

'Ma feet hurt, sir.'

'Well, so do mine, occasionally. Still, you know best. Over yonder, now, trying to hide at the far end of the corridor, that's McAuslan, the dirtiest soldier in the world. In your platoon, by the way. Don't know what to do with McAuslan. Cremation's probably the answer. Nothing else seems to work. Morning, Patterson, what did the MO say?'

'Gave me some gentian violent, sir, tae rub on.'

'Marvellous stuff,' said Bennet-Bruce, with enthusiasm. 'Never travel without it myself. Now, let's see, Ten platoon room over there, Eleven in there, and Twelve round there. Yours is Twelve. Good bunch. Good sergeant, chap called Telfer. Very steady. Meet him in a minute. No, Rafferty, not like that. Give it here.'

We were at a barrack-room door, and a dark, wiry soldier at the first bed was cleaning his rifle, hauling the pullthrough along the barrel. 'Not like that,' said Bennet-Bruce. 'Pull it straight out, not at an angle, or you'll wear away the muzzle and your bullets will fly off squint, missing the enemy, who will seize the opportunity to unseam you, from nave to chaps.' He tugged at the pullthrough. 'What the hell have you got on the end of this, the battalion colours?'

'Piece of four-by-two, sir,' said Rafferty. 'An' a bit o' wire gauze.'

'Who authorized the gauze?'

'Eh, Ah got it fae the store,' said Rafferty uneasily.

'Take it back,' said Bennet-Bruce, 'and never, never use it without the armourer's permission. You know that, don't you? Next time you'll be in Company office. Carry on. I really do despair, sometimes. Morning, Gray. Morning Soutar. Now, let's see.' He stopped at the company noticeboard. ' "Team to play A Company". Good God, you've got me on the right-wing, Corporal Stevenson. That means that

Forbes here will bully and upbraid me through the entire game. I don't really think we're the best thing since Matthews and Carter, do you, Forbes?'

'Just stay on yer wing,' said the saturnine Forbes. 'Ah'll pit the ba' in front of you.'

'Well, I rely on you,' said Bennet-Bruce, passing on. 'That chap Forbes is a marvellous footballer,' he went on to me. 'Signed by Hearts, I understand. You play football? Good show. Of course, that's the great game. The battalion team are district champions, really super team they are, too. Morning, Duff . . .'

And so on. Bennet-Bruce was at home. Finally, he introduced me to Sergeant Telfer, a sturdy, solid-looking man in his mid-thirties who said very little, and left us to get acquainted. This consisted of going over the nominal roll, meeting the corporals, and making polite remarks on my part; obviously if I didn't make the running we would have long silences. However, it seemed to be going well enough for a start.

Next day came that first inspection, and after that the routine drills and exercises, and learning people's names, and getting into the company routine. I worked rather cautiously, by the book, tried a joke or two without response, and told myself it was early days yet. They were a better platoon than I had expected; they were aged round about twenty, a year younger than I was, they were good on drill, did a fifteen-mile route march in five hours without any sign of distress, and on the rifle range were really impressive. But they were not what could be called forthcoming; off parade they were cheery enough with each other, but within my orbit they fell quiet, stolid and watchful.

As I say, I don't know what I expected, but I began to feel depressed. There was something missing; they did what they were told smartly — well, fairly smartly; they took no liberties that I noticed. But if they didn't dislike me they certainly didn't seem to like me either. Perhaps it was my fault; they were happy enough with Bennet-Bruce and any other Company officers who came into contact with them. I envied Macmillan, the subaltern of Ten platoon, who had been in the battalion about six months and abused his platoon good-naturedly one minute and tore strips off them the next; they seemed to get on with him. I wondered if I was the Tiberius type ('let them hate me so long as they fear me'), and concluded I wasn't; it seemed more likely that the Selection Board who took me out of the ranks had just been wrong.

In the mess, things went fairly well until one evening I knocked a pint glass accidentally off the arm of a chair, and a liverish major blasted my clumsiness and observed that there were only about half a dozen of those glasses left. I apologized, red-faced but faintly angry; we looked at each other with mutual dislike, and the trivial incident stuck in my mind. Other things were prickling vaguely, too; my service dress wasn't a good fit, and I knew it. I suspected (wrongly) that this gave rise to covert amusement and once this tiny seed had taken root I was halfway to seeing myself as a laughing-stock.

This can be a dreadful thing to the young, and not only the young. In no time at all I was positive that my platoon found me faintly ridiculous; occasionally I caught what I thought was a glint of amusement in an eye on parade, or heard a stifled laugh. I would tell myself I just imagined these things, but then the doubts would return.

One morning there was a platoon rifle inspection, and I must have been on the down-swing, because I went on it half-conscious of a resolve to put somebody on a charge for something. This, of course, was a deplorable attitude. I had never charged anyone yet, and I may have felt that I ought to, *pour encourager* the platoon in general. Anyway, when I came to a rifle in the middle rank that seemed to have dirt in the grooves of the barrel, I nailed its owner.

He was a nondescript man called Leishman, rather older than the others, a quiet enough character. He seemed genuinely shocked when I told him his rifle was dirty, and then I turned to Sergeant Telfer and said, 'Put him on a charge.' (Six months later I would have said, 'Leishman, did you shave this morning?' And he, dumbfounded, knowing his chin was immaculate, would have said, 'Yes, sir. I did, sir.' And I would have said, 'Of course you did, and it's all gone down the barrel of your gun. Clean the thing.' And that would have been that.)

I went off parade feeling vaguely discontented, and ten minutes later, in the company office, Cormack the clerk observed that I had shaken Leishman, no mistake. He said it deadpan, and added that Leishman was presently in the armoury, cleaning his rifle. Puzzled, for I wondered why Cormack should be telling me this, I went off to the armoury.

Sure enough, there was Leishman, pulling the cleaning-cloth through his rifle, and crying. He was literally weeping. I was shocked.

'What's the matter?' I said, for this was a new one to me.

He snuffled a bit, and wiped his nose, and then it came out. He had been five years in the Army, his discharge was coming up in a few weeks, he had never been on a charge in his life before. He was going to have his clean sheet marred almost on the eve of getting out.

'Well, for God's sake,' I said, relieved more than anything else. 'Look, don't get into a state. It's all right, we'll scrub the charge.' I was quite glad to, because I felt a warning would have done. 'I'm certainly not going to spoil your record,' I said.

He mumped some more, and pulled his rifle through again.

'Let's have a look at it,' I said. I looked down the barrel, and it still wasn't all that good, but what would you? He was obviously badly upset, but he muttered something about thanks, which just made me uncomfortable. I suppose born leaders don't find authority embarrassing.

'Forget it,' I said. 'Give it another few pullsthrough, and keep your eye on it until your ticket comes through. Okay?'

I left him to it, and about ten minutes later I was passing the door of Twelve platoon barrack-room, and heard somebody laughing inside. I just glanced as I went by, and stopped short. It was Leishman, sitting on his bunk at the far end, laughing with a bunch of his mates.

I moved on a few steps. All right, he had made a quick recovery. He was relieved. There was nothing in that. But he had seemed really upset in the armoury, shaken, as Cormack said. Now he was roaring his head off – the quality of laughter somehow caught the edge of my nerves. I stood undecided, and then wheeled round and shouted:

'Sergeant Telfer!'

He came out of his room. 'Yessir?'

'Sergeant Telfer,' I said, 'stop that man laughing.'

He gaped at me. 'Laughing, sir?'

'Yes, laughing. Tell him to stop it – now.'

'But ...' he looked bewildered. 'But ... he's just laughin', sir ...'

'I know he's just laughing. He's braying his bloody head off. Tell him to stop it.'

'Right, sir.' He obviously thought the sun had got me, but he strode into the barrack-room. Abruptly, Leishman's laughter stopped, then there was what might have been a smothered chuckle, then silence.

Feeling suicidal, I went back to my billet. Obviously Leishman had thought I was a mug; I should have let the charge stick. Let someone get away with it, even a good soldier, and you have taken some of his virtue away. On the other hand, maybe he had been laughing about something else entirely; in that case, I had been an idiot to give Sergeant Telfer that ridiculous order. Either way, I looked a fool. And my Service dress didn't fit. To hell with it. I would see the adjutant tomorrow and ask for a posting.

I didn't, of course. That night in the mess the liverish major, of all people, asked me to partner him in a ludo doubles against the adjutant and the MO. (In stations where diversion is limited games like ludo tend to get elevated above their usual status.) In spite of the MO's constant gamesmanship, directed against my partner's internal condition, we won by one counter in a grandstand finish, and thereafter it was a happy evening. We finished with a sing-song – *Massacre of Macpherson* and *The Lum Hat Wantin' the Croon*, and other musical gems – and the result was that I went to bed thinking that the world could be worse, after all.

In the morning when I inspected my platoon, Sergeant Telfer did not roll on the ground, helpless with laughter, at the sight of me. If anything, the platoon was smarter and faster than usual; I inspected the rifles, and Leishman's was gleaming as though he had used Brasso on the barrel, which he quite probably had. I said nothing; there was no hint that the incident of yesterday had ever happened.

On the other hand, there was still no sign of the happy officer–man relationship by which the manual sets such store. We were still at a distance with each other, and so it continued. It didn't matter whether I criticized or praised, the reception was as wary as ever.

Remembering the CO's advice, I had reached the stage where I knew every man by name, and had picked up a few nicknames as well. Brown, a clueless, lanky Glaswegian, was Daft Bob; Forbes, the villainous-looking footballer, was Heinie (after Heinrich Himmler, it transpired); my own batman, McClusky, was Chick; and Leishman was Soapy. But others I had not yet identified – Pudden, and Jeep, and Darkie, and Hi-Hi; one heard the names shouted along the company corridors and floating through the barrack-room doors – 'Jeep's away for ile* the day', which signified that the mysterious Jeep was *hors de combat*, physically or spiritually; 'Darkie's got a rare hatchet on', meaning that Darkie was in a bad temper; 'yon Heinie's a wee bramar', which was the highest sort of compliment,

* Ile = oil (castor oil).

and so on. It was interesting stuff, but it was still rather like studying the sounds of a strange species; I couldn't claim to be with it.

My own batman, McClusky, reflected the situation. He was a good worker, and my kit was always in excellent condition, but whereas with his mates he was a cheery, rather waggish soul, with me he was as solemn as a Free Kirk elder. He was a round, tousled lad with a happy pug face and a stream of 'Glasgow patter' which dried up at the door of my room and thereafter became a series of monosyllabic grunts.

Well, I thought, this is the way it's going to be, and it could be worse. If I couldn't like them, yet, I could at least respect them, for they were a good platoon; when Bennet-Bruce held his full-dress monthly inspection for the Colonel, the great man was pleased to say that Twelve platoon's kit layout was the best in the battalion. It should have been; they had worked hard enough. Having been, for a time at least, in the Indian Army, I had my own ideas about how kit should be laid out; I had taken aside Fletcher, the platoon dandy, and shown him how I thought it should be presented for inspection – if you black the soles of your boots, for example, they look better, and a little square of red and white four-by-two cloth under an oil-bottle and pullthrough is smarter than nothing at all. Fletcher had watched me stonily as I went over his kit, but afterwards he had supervised the whole room in laying out their stuff on the same pattern. Our one problem had been what to do with Private McAuslan, the dirtiest soldier in the world; I solved that by sending him into town for the day as guard on the company truck, which had nothing in it anyway. His kit was placed in an out-of-the-way cupboard, his associates affecting to be disgusted by the mere sight of it, and securely locked up.

Anyway, the Colonel limped through, inspecting and approving, and when he had gone and the quiet, involuntary sigh had sounded through the big, whitewashed room,

I said, 'Nice show, sons.' But none of them made any comment, so I left them to it.

About two days later, which was shortly before Christmas, I fell from grace in the mess. There was a mess meeting called, and I forgot about it, and went into town to play snooker at the Officers' Club. As a result I got a nasty dig next day from the adjutant, and was told that I was orderly officer for the whole of next week; normally you do orderly officer only a day at a time.

This was a nuisance, since the orderly officer has to stay in barracks, but the worst of it was that I would miss the great Hogmanay party on New Year's Eve. To Highlanders, of course, Christmas is a pagan festival which they are perfectly prepared to enjoy as long as no one sees them doing it, but Hogmanay is the night of the year. Then they sing and drink and eat and drink and reminisce and drink, and the New Year comes in in a tartan, whisky-flavoured haze. The regimental police shut up shop, haggis is prepared in quantity, black bun is baked, the padre preaches a sermon reminding everyone that New Year is a time for rededication ('ye can say that again, meenister', murmurs a voice at the back), and the sergeants extend their annual invitation to the officers.

This is the great event. The Colonel forms the officers up as a platoon, and marches them to the sergeants' mess, where they are greeted with the singing of *We are Fred Karno's Army*, or some other appropriate air, and the festivities go on until well into the next morning. The point was that the sergeants' mess was outside barracks, so as orderly officer I would be unable to attend.

Not that I minded, particularly, but it would be a very silent, sober night in barracks all by myself, and even if you are not a convivial type, when you are in a Scottish regiment you feel very much out of it if you are on your own on Hogmanay. Anyway, there it was; I mounted my guards and inspected my cookhouses during that week, and on December 31st I had had about enough of it. The battalion was on holiday; the Jocks were preparing to invade the town *en masse* ('there'll be a rerr terr in the toon the night', I heard McClusky remarking to one of the other batmen), and promptly at seven o'clock the Colonel marched off the officers, every one dressed in his best, for the sergeants' mess.

After they had gone, I strolled across the empty parade ground in the dusk, and mooched around the deserted company offices. I decided that the worst bit of it was that every Jock in the battalion knew that the new subaltern was on defaulters, and therefore an object of pity and derision. Having thought this, I promptly rebuked myself for self-pity, and whistled all the way back to my quarters.

I heard Last Post at ten o'clock, watched the first casualty of the night being helped into the cells, saw that the guard were reasonably sober, and returned to my room. There was nothing to do now until about 4 AM, when I would inspect the picquets, so I climbed into my pyjamas and into bed, setting my alarm clock on the side-table. I smoked a little, and read a little, and dozed a little, and from time to time very distant sounds of revelry drifted through the African night. The town would be swinging on its hinges, no doubt.

It must have been about midnight that I heard feet on the gravel outside, and a muttering of voices in the dark. There was a clinking noise which indicated merrymakers, but they were surprisingly quiet considering the occasion. The footsteps came into the building, and up the corridor, and there was a knock on my door.

I switched on the light and opened up. There were five of them, dressed in the best tartans they had put on for Hogmanay. There was McClusky, my batman, Daft Bob Brown, Fletcher of the wooden countenance, Forbes, and Leishman. Brown carried a paper bag which obviously contained bottles, and Forbes had a carton of beer under his arm. For a moment we looked at each other.

'Well,' I said at last. 'Hullo.'

Then we looked at each other some more, in silence, while I wondered what this was in aid of, and then I searched for something further to say – the situation was fairly unusual. Finally I said,

'Won't you come in?'

They filed in, Daft Bob almost dropping the bottles and being rebuked in hideous terms by Fletcher. I closed the door, and said wouldn't they sit down, and Leishman and Daft Bob sat on my room-mate's bed, Fletcher placed himself on the only chair, and Forbes and McClusky sat on the floor. They looked sidelong at each other.

'Well,' I said. 'This is nice.'

There was a pause, and then Fletcher said,

'Uh-huh.'

I thought furiously for something to say. 'Er, I thought you were going into the town, McClusky?'

He looked sheepish. 'Ach, the toon. Naethin' doin'. Deid quiet.'

'Wisnae bad, though, at the Blue Heaven,' said Daft Bob. 'Some no' bad jiggin'.' (Dancing, that is).

'Ach, jiggin',' said Fletcher contemptuously. 'Nae talent in this toon.'

'I'm sorry,' I said, conscious that in these unusual circumstances I was nevertheless the host. 'I don't have anything ...'

'... in the hoose,' said Leishman unexpectedly, and we laughed.

'No' tae worry,' said Fletcher. He slapped Daft Bob sharply on the knee. 'C'mon, you. Gie the man a drink.'

'Comin' up,' said Daft Bob, and produced a bottle of beer from his bag. He held it out to me.

'In the name o' the wee man,' said Fletcher. 'Where the hell were you brought up? Gie 'im a glass, ya mug.'

Daft Bob said, 'Ach!' and rummaged for tumblers, McClusky came to his assistance, and Fletcher abused them both, striking them sharply about the knees and wrists. Finally we were all provided for, and Fletcher said,

'Aye, weel, here's tae us.'

'Wha's like us?' said McClusky.

'Dam' few,' said Forbes.

'And they're a' deid,' I said, completing the ritual.

'Aw-haw-hey,' said Daft Bob and we drank.

Conversationally, I asked: 'What brought you over this way?'

They grinned at each other, and Forbes whistled the bugle call 'You can be a defaulter as long as you like as long as you answer your na-a-a-me.' They all chuckled and shook their heads.

I understood. In my own way, I was on defaulters.

'Fill them up, ye creature ye,' said Fletcher to Daft Bob, and this time Daft Bob, producing more glasses from his bag, gave us whisky as well. It occurred to me that the penalty for an officer drinking in his own billet with enlisted men was probably death, or the equivalent, but frankly, if Montgomery himself had appeared in the doorway I couldn't have cared less.

'They're fair gaun it up at the sergeants' mess,' said Forbes. 'Ah heard the adjutant singing *Roll me over*.'

'Sair heids the morn,' said McClusky primly.

'The Jeep'll be away for ile again,' said Leishman.

'The Jeep?' I said.

'Captain Bennet-Bruce,' said Fletcher. 'Your mate.'

'Oh,' I said.

'Stoap cuddlin' that bottle tae yerself as if it wis Wee Willie, the collier's dyin' child,' said Fletcher to Daft Bob.

'Ye'd think you'd paid for it,' said Daft Bob, indignantly. 'Honest, sir, d'ye hear him? Ah hate him. I do.'

They snarled at each other, happily, and the quiet Forbes shook his head at me as over wayward children. We refilled the glasses, and I handed round cigarettes, and a few minutes later we were refilling them again, and Leishman, tapping his foot on the floor, was starting to hum gently. McClusky, after an anxious glance at me, took it up, and they sang *The Muckin' o' Geordie's Byre* — for Leishman was an Aberdonian, and skilled in that strange tongue.

'That's a right teuchter song,' said Fletcher, and gave tongue:

> *As I gaed doon tae Wilson Toon*
> *Ah met wee Geordie Scobie,*
> *Says he tae me 'Could ye gang a hauf?'*
> *Says I, 'Man, that's my hobby.'*

We came in quietly on the chorus, which is 'We're no awa' to bide awa', we'll aye come back and see ye,' which Scottish soldiers invariably sing after the first two or three drinks, and which the remnants of the regiment had sung as they waited for the end at St Valery. Then we refilled them again, and while Fletcher and Daft Bob wrangled over the distribution, Forbes asked me with casual unconcern how I was liking the battalion. I said I liked it very well, and we talked of this and that, of platoon business and how the Rangers were doing, and the Glasgow police force and the North African weather. And after a few more drinks, in strict sobriety, Fletcher said:

'We'll have tae be gettin' along.'

'Not a bit of it,' I said. 'It's not late.'

'Aye, weel,' said Fletcher, 'mebbe it's no'.'

'Aw-haw-hey,' said Daft Bob.

So another half-hour passed, and I wondered how I would find out the answers to the questions which could not be asked. Probably I wouldn't, but it didn't matter, anyway. Next day, on parade, Fletcher would be looking to his front as stonily as ever, Leishman would have given several extra minutes' attention to his rifle, I would be addressing Daft Bob severely, and all would be as it had been — except that for some reason they had thought it worthwhile to come and see me on Hogmanay. Some things you don't ponder over; you are just glad they happened.

'You gaunae sit boozin' a' night?' Fletcher snapped at Daft Bob. 'Sup, sup, sup, takin' it in like a sponge. I'm ashamed o' ye'.'

'Ah'll no' be rollin' in your gutter, Fletcher,' said Daft Bob. 'So ye neednae worry. It's no' me Mr MacNeill'll be peggin' in' the mornin' for no' bein' able tae staun up on parade.'

'Peg the baith o' ye,' said Forbes. 'Ye're aye greetin' at each other.'

'Sharrup,' said Fletcher. 'C'mon, get the bottles packed up. Let the man get tae his bed.'

Daft Bob and McClusky collected the empties, while Fletcher bossed them, and they all straightened their bonnets, and looked at each other again.

'Aye, weel,' said Forbes.

'Well,' I said, and stopped. Some things are impossible to put into words. 'Well,' I said again. 'It was great to see you. Thank you for coming.'

'Ye'll be seein' us again,' said Fletcher.

'Aw-haw-hey,' said Daft Bob.

'Every mornin', numbered aff by the right, eh, Heinie?' said McClusky.

'That's the way,' said Forbes.

'Tallest on the right, shortest on the left.'

'Clean, bright, and slightly oiled.'

'We're the wee boys.'

'Gi' the ba' tae the man wi' glasses.'

'Here's tae us, wha's like us?'

'Aw-haw-hey.'

'Ye gaunae staun' there a' night, then?' demanded Fletcher.

'Ah'm gaun. Ah'm gaun,' said Daft Bob. 'Night, sir. Guid New Year.' They jostled out, saying goodnight and a good New Year, and exchanging their incredible slogans.

'Goodnight,' I said. 'Thanks again. Goodnight, Fletcher.

Goodnight, Forbes. Goodnight, Daf—, er, Brown. Good-night.'

They clattered off up the corridor, and I closed the door. The room was full of cigarette smoke and bar-room smell, the ashtrays were overflowing, and there was a quarter-full bottle of whisky still on the side-table, forgotten in the packing. I sat on the edge of my bed feeling about twenty feet tall.

Their feet sounded on the gravel, and I heard Daft Bob muttering, and being rebuked, as usual, by Fletcher.

'Sharrup, ye animal.'

'Ah'll no' sharrup. Ah'll better go back an' get it; it was near half-full.'

'Ach, Chick'll get it in the mornin'.'

There was a doubt-laden pause, and then Daft Bob: 'D'ye think it'll be there in the mornin'?'

'Ach, for the love o' the wee wheel!' exclaimed Fletcher. 'Are ye worried aboot yer wee bottle? Yer ain, wee totty bottle? Ye boozy bum, ye! D'ye think Darkie's gaun tae lie there a' night sookin' at yer miserable bottle? C'mon, let's get tae wir kips.'

The sound of their footsteps faded away, and I climbed back into bed. In addition to everything else, I had found out who Darkie was.

Play up, Play up
and Get Tore in

THE native Highlanders, the Englishmen, and the Low-landers played football on Saturday afternoons and talked about it on Saturday evenings, but the Glaswegians, men apart in this as in most things, played, slept, ate, drank, and lived it seven days a week. Some soldiering they did because even a peace-time battalion in North Africa makes occasional calls on its personnel, but that was incidental; they were just waiting for the five minutes when they could fall out crying: 'Haw, Wully, sees a ba'.'

From the moment when the drums beat *Johnnie Cope* at sunrise until it became too dark to see in the evening, the steady thump-thump of a boot on a ball could be heard somewhere in the barracks. It was tolerated because there was no alternative; even the parade ground was not sacred from the small shuffling figures of the Glasgow men, their bonnets pulled down over their eyes, kicking, trapping, swerving and passing, and occasionally intoning, like ugly little high priests, their ritual cries of 'Way-ull' and 'Aw-haw-hey'. The simile is apt, for it was almost a religious exercise, to be interrupted only if the Colonel happened to stroll by. Then they would wait, relaxed, one of them with the ball underfoot, until the majestic figure had gone past, flicking his brow in acknowledgement, and at the soft signal, 'Right, Wully,' the ball would be off again.

I used to watch them wheeling like gulls, absorbed in their wonderful fitba'. They weren't in Africa or the Army any longer; in imagination they were running on the green turf of Ibrox or Paradise, hearing instead of bugle calls the rumble and roar of a hundred thousand voices; this was their common daydream, to play (according to religion) either for Celtic or Rangers. All except Daft Bob Brown, the battalion idiot; in his fantasy he was playing for Partick Thistle.

They were frighteningly skilful. As sports officer I was expected actually to play the game, and I have shameful recollections still of a Company practice match in which I was pitted against a tiny, wizened creature who in happier days had played wing-half for Bridgeton Waverley. What a monkey he made out of me. He was quicksilver with a glottal stop, nipping past, round, and away from me, trailing the ball tantalizingly close and magnetizing it away again. The only reason he didn't run between my legs was that he didn't think of it. It could have been bad for discipline, but it wasn't. When he was making me look the the biggest clown since Grock I wasn't his platoon commander any more; I was just an opponent to beat.

With all this talent to choose from – the battalion was seventy-five per cent Glasgow men – it followed that the regimental team was something special. In later years more than half of them went on to play for professional teams, and one was capped for Scotland, but never in their careers did they have the opportunity for perfecting their skill that they had in that battalion. They were young and as fit as a recent war had made them; they practised together constantly in a Mediterranean climate; they had no worries; they loved their game. At their peak, when they were murdering the opposition from Tobruk to the Algerian border, they were a team that could have given most club sides in the world a little trouble, if nothing more.

The Colonel didn't speak their language, but his attitude to them was more than one of paternal affection for his soldiers. He respected their peculiar talent, and would sit in the stand at games crying 'Play up!' and 'Oh, dear,

McIlhatton!' When they won, as they invariably did, he would beam and patronize the other colonels, and when they brought home the Command Cup he was almost as proud as he was of the Battle Honours.

In his pride he became ambitious. 'Look, young Dand,' he said. 'Any reason why they shouldn't go on tour? You know, round the Med, play the garrison teams, eh? I mean, they'd win, wouldn't they?'

I said they ought to be far too strong for most regimental sides.

'Good, good,' he said, full of the spirit that made British sportsmanship what it is. 'Wallop the lot of them, excellent. Right, I'll organize it.'

When the Colonel organized something, it was organized; within a couple of weeks I was on my way to the docks armed with warrants and a suitcase full of cash, and in the back of the truck were the battalion team, plus reserves, all beautiful in their best tartans, sitting with their arms folded and their bonnets, as usual, over their faces.

When I lined them up on the quayside, preparatory to boarding one of HM coastal craft, I was struck again by their lack of size. They were extremely neat men, as Glaswegians usually are, quick, nervous, and deft as monkeys, but they were undoubtedly small. A century of life – of living, at any rate – in the hell's kitchen of industrial Glasgow, has cut the stature and mighty physique of the Scotch-Irish people pitifully; Glasgow is full of little men today, but at least they are stouter and sleeker than my team was. They were the children of the hungry Thirties, hard-eyed and wiry; only one of them was near my size, a fair, dreamy youth called McGlinchy, one of the reserves. He was a useless, beautiful player, a Stanley Matthews for five minutes of each game, and for the rest of the time an indolent passenger who strolled about the left wing, humming to himself. Thus he was normally in the second eleven. ('He's got fitba',' the corporal who captained the first team would say, 'but whit the hell, he's no' a' there; he's wandered.')

The other odd man out in the party was Private Mc-Auslan, the dirtiest soldier in the world, who acted as lines-man and baggage-master, God help us. The Colonel had wanted to keep him behind, and send someone more fit for human inspection, but the team had protested violently. They were just men, and McAuslan was their linesman, foul as he was. In fairness I had backed them up, and now I was regretting it, for McAuslan is not the kind of orna-ment that you want to advertise your team in Mediter-ranean capitals. He stood there with the baggage, grimy and dishevelled, showing a tasteful strip of grey vest be-tween kilt and tunic, and with his hosetops wrinkling to-wards his ankles.

'All right, children,' I said, 'get aboard,' and as they chat-tered up the gangplank I went to look for the man in charge. I found him in a passageway below decks, leaning with his forehead against a pipe, singing *The Ash Grove* and fuming of gin. I addressed him, and he looked at me. Possibly the sight of a man in Highland dress was too much for him, what with the heat, for he put his hands over his eyes and said, 'Oh dear, oh dear,' but I convinced him that I was real, and he came to quite briskly. We got off to a fine start with the following memorable exchange.

Me: Excuse me, can you tell me when this boat starts?

He: It's not a boat, it's a ship.

Me: Oh, sorry. Well have you any idea, when it starts?

He: If I hadn't, I wouldn't be the bloody captain, would I?

Now that we were chatting like old friends, I introduced myself. He was a Welshman, stocky and middle-aged, with the bland, open face of a cherub and a heart as black as Satan's waistcoat. His name was Samuels, and he was very evil, as I discovered. At the moment, he was not pleased to see me, but he offered me gin, muttering about the in-dignity of having his fine vessel used as a floating hotel for

a lot of blasted pongoes, and Scotch pongoes at that. I excused myself, went to see that my Highlanders were com-
fortably installed – I found them ranged solemnly on a
platform in the engine room, looking at the engines – and
having shepherded them to their quarters and prevented
McAuslan falling over the side, I went to my cabin. There
I counted the money – it was a month's pay for the party
– and before I had finished the ship began to vibrate and
we were away, like Hannibal, to invade the North.

I am no judge of naval behaviour, but looking back I
should say that if the much-maligned William Bligh had
been half as offensive as Lieutenant Samuels the *Bounty*
would never have got the length of Land's End, let alone
Tahiti. At the first meal in the ward-room – which consisted for him of gin and chocolate biscuits – he snarled at
his officers, bullied the stewards, and cross-examined me
with a hackle-raising mixture of contempt and curiosity.
We were going to the Grand Island, he knew; and what did
we think we were going to do there? Play football, was it?
Was that all pongoes had to do? And who were we going
to play, then?

Keeping my temper I told him we had several matches
arranged against Service and civilian teams on the island,
and he chose to make light of our chances. He had seen
my team aboard; they were midgets, and anyway who had
they ever beaten?

At this one of his officers said he had seen us play, and
we were good, very good. Samuels glared at him, but later
he became thoughtful, applying himself to his gin, and
when the meal ended he was still sitting there, brooding
darkly. His officers looked nervous; they seemed to know
the signs.

Next morning the African coast was still in view. I was
surprised enough to ask Samuels about this, and he laughed
and looked at me slantendicular.

'We're not goin' straight to the Island, Jocko,' he explained. 'Got to look in at Derna first, to pick up supplies.

Don't worry, it won't take long.' He seemed oddly excited, but distinctly pleased with himself.

I didn't mind, and when Samuels suggested that we take the opportunity to go ashore at Derna so that my boys could have a practice kick-about, I was all for it. He went further; having vanished mysteriously into the town to conclude his official business, he returned to say that he was in a position to fix up a practice match against the local garrison side — 'thought you boys might like a try-out against some easy opposition, like; some not bad footballers yere, give you a game, anyway.'

Since we had several hours before we sailed it seemed not a bad idea; I consulted with the corporal-captain, and we told Samuels to go ahead. And then things started happening.

First of all, Samuels suggested we change into football kit on the ship. There was nothing odd about that, but when we went to the baggage-room the team's fine yellow jerseys with the little tartan badge were missing; it transpired that through some inexplicable mix-up they were now in the ship's laundry, being washed. Not to worry, said Samuels, we'll lend you some blue shirts, which he did.

He took personal charge of our party when we went ashore — I was playing myself, as it was an unimportant game, and I wanted to rest our left-half, who had been slightly seasick. We played on a mud-baked pitch near the harbour, and coasted to a very gentle 7–o win. Afterwards the garrison team invited us for drinks and supper, but Samuels interrupted my acceptance to say we hadn't time; we had to catch the tide, or the wind, or something, and we were bundled into the truck and hurried back to the harbour. But one remark the garrison captain let fall in parting, and it puzzled me.

'It's odd,' he said, 'to find so many Scotsmen in one ship's crew.'

I mentioned this to Samuels, back on board, and he sniggered wickedly.

'Well, now, natural enuff,' he said. 'He thought you was all in the ship's company.'

A horrid suspicion was forming in my mind as I asked him to explain.

'Well, see now,' he said, 'I 'ad an idea. When I went ashore first, I looks in on the garrison an' starts talkin' football. "Got a pretty fair team yere, 'avent you?" I says. "District champions," says they. "Couldn't beat my ship's company," I says – cuttin' a long story short, you understand. "Couldn't what?" says they. "You want to bet?" says I.' He sat back, beaming wickedly at me. 'So I got on a little bet.'

I gaped at the man. 'You mean you passed off my team, under false pretences ... You little shark! You could get the jail for this.'

'Grow up, boyo,' said Samuels. 'Lissen, it's a gold mine. I was just tryin' it out before lettin' you in. Look, we can't go wrong. We can clean up the whole coast, an' then you can do your tour on the Island. Who knows your Jocks aren't my matelots? And they'll bite every time; what's a mingy little coaster, they'll say, it can't have no football team.' He cackled and drank gin. 'Oh, boy! They don't know we've got the next best thing to the Arsenal on board!'

'Right,' I said. 'Give me the money you won.' He stared at me. 'It's going back to the garrison,' I explained.

'You gone nuts, boyo?'

'No, I haven't. Certainly not nuts enough to let you get away with using my boys, my regiment, dammit, to feather your little nest. Come on, cough up.'

But he wouldn't, and the longer we argued the less it seemed I could do anything about it. To expose the swindle would be as embarrassing for me and my team as for Samuels. So in the end I had to drop it, and got some satisfaction from telling him that it was his first and last killing as far as we were concerned. He cursed a bit, for he had planned the most plunderous operation seen in the Med since the Barbary corsairs, but later he brightened up.

'I'll still win a packet on you on the Island,' he said. 'You're good, Jocko. Them boys of yours are the sweetest thing this side of Ninian Park. Football is an art, is it? But you're missin' a great opportunity. I thought Scotsmen were sharp, too.'

That disposed of, it was a pleasant enough voyage, marred only by two fights between McAuslan on the one hand and members of the crew, who had criticised his unsanitary appearance, on the other. I straightened them out, upbraided McAuslan, and instructed him how to behave.

'You're a guest, you horrible article,' I said. 'Be nice to the sailors; they are your friends. Fraternize with them; they were on our side in the war, you know? And for that matter, when we get to the Island, I shall expect a higher standard than ever from all of you. Be a credit to the regiment, and keep moderately sober after the games. Above all, don't fight. Cut out the Garscube Road stuff or I'll blitz you.'

Just how my simple, manly words affected them you could see from the glazed look in their eyes, and I led them down the gangplank at Grand Island feeling just a mite apprehensive. They were good enough boys, but as wild as the next, and it was more than usually important that they keep out of trouble because the Military Governor, who had been instrumental in fixing the tour, was formerly of a Highland regiment, and would expect us not only to win our games but to win golden opinions for deportment.

He was there to meet us, with aides and minions, a stately man of much charm who shook hands with the lads and then departed in a Rolls, having assured me that he was going to be at every game. Then the Press descended on us, I was interviewed about our chances, and we were all lined up and photographed. The result, as seen in the evening paper, was mixed. The team were standing there in their kilts, frowning suspiciously, with me at one end grinning inanely. At the other end crouched an anthropoid figure, dressed apparently in old sacking; at first I thought an Arab mendicant had strayed into the picture, but closer inspection identified it as McAuslan showing, as one of the team remarked, his good side.

Incidentally, it seemed from the paper's comments that we were not highly rated. The hint seemed to be that we were being given a big build-up simply because we were from the Governor's old brigade, but that when the garrison teams – and I knew they were good teams – got us, we would be pretty easy meat. This suited me, and it obviously didn't worry the team. They were near enough professional to know that games aren't won in newspaper columns.

We trained for two days and had our first game against the German prisoners-of-war. They were men still waiting to be repatriated, ex-Africa Korps, big and tough, and they had played together since they went into the bag in '42. Some of our team wore the Africa Star, and you could feel the tension higher than usual in the dressing-room beforehand. The corporal, dapper and wiry, stamped his boots on the concrete, bounced the ball, and said, 'Awright fellas, let's get stuck intae these Huns,' and out they trotted.

(I should say at this point that this final exhortation varied only according to our opponents. Years later, when he led a famous league side out to play Celtic, this same corporal, having said his Hail Mary and fingered his crucifix, instructed his team, 'Awright, fellas, let's get stuck intae these Papes.' There is a lesson in team spirit there, if you think about it.)

The Germans were good, but not good enough. They were clever for their size, but our boys kept the ball down and the game close, and ran them into a sweat before half-

time. We should have won by about four clear goals, but
the breaks didn't come, and we had to be content with
2–0. Personally I was exhausted: I had had to sit beside
the Governor, who had played rugby, but if I had tried to
explain the finer points he wouldn't have heard them anyway. He worked himself into a state of nervous frenzy,
wrenching his handkerchief in his fingers and giving an-
tique yelps of 'Off your side!' and 'We claim foul!' which
contrasted oddly with the raucous support of our reserve
players, whose repertoire was more varied and included
'Dig a hole for 'im!', 'Sink 'im!' and the inevitable 'Get
tore intae these people!' At the end the Germans cried
'Hoch! hoch!' and we gave three cheers, and both sides
came off hating each other.

Present in body and also in raw spirit was Lieutenant
Samuels, who accosted me after the game with many a
wink and leer. It seemed he had cleaned up again.

'An' I'll tell you, boyo, I'll do even better. The Artillery
beat the Germans easy, so they figure to be favourites
against you. But I seen your boys playin' at half-steam today. We'll murder 'em.' He nudged me. 'Want me to get a
little bet on for you, hey? Money for old rope, man.'

Knowing him, I seemed to understand Sir Henry Morgan
and Lloyd George better than I had ever done.

So the tour progressed, and the Island sat up a little
straighter with each game. We came away strongly
against the Engineers, 6–0, beat the top civilian team 3–0,
and on one of those dreadful off-days just scraped home
against the Armoured Corps, 1—0. It was scored by Mc-
Glinchy, playing his first game and playing abysmally.
Then late on he ambled on to a loose ball on the edge of
the penalty circle, tossed the hair out of his eyes, flicked
the ball from left foot to right to left without letting it
touch the ground, and suddenly unleashed the most un-
holy piledriver you ever saw. It hit the underside of the
bar from twenty-five yards out and glanced into the net
with the goalkeeper standing still, and you could almost

hear McGlinchy sigh as he trotted back absently to his wing, scratching his ear.

'Wandered!' said the corporal bitterly afterwards. 'Away wi' the fairies! He does that, and for the rest o' the game he micht as well be in his bed. He's a genius, sir, but no' near often enough. Ye jist daurnae risk 'im again.'

I agreed with him. So far we hadn't lost a goal, and although I had no illusions about preserving that record, I was beginning to hope that we would get through the tour unbeaten. The Governor, whose excitement was increasing with every game, was heard to express the opinion that we were the sharpest thing in the whole Middle East; either he was getting pot-valiant or hysterical, I wasn't sure which, but he went about bragging at dinners until his commanders got sick of him, and us.

But the public liked us, and so did the Press, and when we took the Artillery to the cleaners, 3–2, in one of the fastest and most frantic games I have ever seen, amateur or pro, they were turning crowds away from the stadium. The Governor was like an antelope full of adrenalin, eating his handkerchief and shivering about in his seat, crying, 'Oh, my goodness gracious me!' and 'Ah, hah, he has, he hasn't, oh my God!' and flopping back, exhausted. I was too busy to steady him; I was watching (it dawned on me) a really fine football team. They moved like a machine out there, my wiry, tireless wee keelies, and it wasn't just their speed, their trickiness, or their accuracy; it was their cool, impregnable assurance. What gets into a man, who is nervous when a sergeant barks at him, but who, when he is put out in front of 20,000 shouting spectators, and asked to juggle an elusive leather ball, reacts with all the poise and certainty of an acrobat on a high wire?

I didn't need to tell them they were good. They knew it, and perhaps some of them knew it too well. Following the Artillery game, two of them got picked up by the MPs, fighting drunk and out of bounds, and I had to pull out all the stops to save their necks. I dropped them from the next game (which we won narrowly, 4–3), and then came our final match, and we won it 4–o, and that was it. I relaxed, the Governor took to his bed for a couple of days, wheezing like a deflating balloon, Lieutenant Samuels danced on the bar at the Officers' Club ('Jocko, boy, you're luv-ley, an' all your little Scotch Pongoes are luv-ley, hoots mon, an' I've won a dirty, great, big, luv-ley packet. You know what? I 'ad all the ships funds as well as my own money on 'em for the Artillery game') and my team took it easy at last. That is to say that during the day they punted the ball about on the practice pitch, crying 'Way-ull' and 'Aw-haw-hey,' and at night they sat in the bars, drinking beer and eyeing the talent, and keeping their bonnets over their eyes.

With the pressure off they drank more and ate more, and I was not surprised when, a few days before we were due to leave the Island, two of them came down with one of those bugs which inhabit melons in foreign parts and give you gyppy tummy, or as they call it in India, Delhi Belly. They were packed off to bed and I read the others a lecture on the perils of over-indulgence. It was good, strong stuff, and so influenced me personally that I declined to join Lieutenant Samuels in the celebratory dinner which he tried to press on me at the Officers' Club that night.

I regarded him with distaste. 'Why aren't you out sinking submarines or something?'

'This is peacetime, boyo,' said he. 'Anyway, we're gettin' a refit; we'll be yere for weeks. I can stand it, I'm tellin' you.' I doubted whether he could; the gin was obviously lapping against his palate and his complexion was like a desert sunrise. He insisted loudly on buying me a drink at least, and I was finishing it and trying not to listen to his gloating account of how he would spend the filthy amount of money he had won, when I was called to the phone.

It was the Governor, excited but brisk. 'MacNeill,' he said. 'How's your team?'

Wondering, I said they were fine.

'Excellent, capital. I think I can arrange another game for them, farewell appearance, y'know. That all right with you?'

I was about to mention the two men in hospital, and that we wouldn't be at full strength, but after all, we were here to play, not to make excuses. So I said, 'Splendid, any time,' and before I could ask about our opponents and the where and when, he had said he would ring me later and hung up.

Samuels, now fully lit, was delighted. 'It never rains but it pours,' he exclaimed gleefully. 'Send it down, David. Let's see, put a packet on your boys – who they playin'? doesn't matter – collect on that, crikee, Jocko, what a killin'! I'll plank the bet first thing . . . trouble is, they're gettin' to know me. Ne'mind, I'll get my clerk to put it on, he can go in mufti.' He crowed and rubbed his hands. 'Luv-ley little pongoes; best cargo I ever had!'

It seemed to me he was taking a lot for granted; after all, our opponents might be somebody really good. But we'd beaten the best in the Island, so he probably couldn't go wrong.

So I thought, until I heard from the Governor's aide late that night. 'Two-thirty, at the Stadium,' he said. 'Full uniform for you, of course, and *do* see, old man, that your Jocks are respectable. Can't you get them to wear their hats on the *tops* of their heads? They tend rather to look like coalmen.'

'Sure, sure. Who are we playing?'

'Mmh? Oh, the other lot? The Fleet.'

For a moment I didn't follow. He explained.

'The Fleet. The Navy. *You* know, chaps in ships with blue trousers.' He began to sing *Heart of Oak*.

'But . . . but . . . but,' I said. 'That's like playing the Army. I mean, there are thousands of them. They'll be all-professional . . . they'll murder us . . . they . . .'

'That's what the Admiral thought,' said the aide, 'but

our Chief wouldn't see it. Got rather excited actually;
they're still arguing in there; can't you hear 'em? Amazing,'
he went on, 'how the Chief's manner changes when he gets
worked up about a thing like this; he sounds positively
Scotch. What's a sumph, by the way?'

I wasn't listening any longer. I was sweating. It wasn't
panic, or the fear of defeat. After all, we had done well,
and no one could expect us to hold the Navy; we would
just have to put on a good show. I was just concentrating
on details – get the boys to bed quickly, two men in hospital,
choose the team, balance it as well as possible. I ran over
the reserves: Beattie, Forbes, McGlinchy, myself . . . Lord,
the Fleet! And I had fourteen to choose from. Well, barring
miracles, we would lose. The Governor would be in mourn-
ing: that was his hard luck, if he didn't know better than
to pit us against a side that would be half First Division
pros, and possibly even an internationalist. Suddenly I felt
elated. Suppose . . . oh, well, we'd give them something to
remember us by.

I simply told the boys at bedtime who they were playing,
and they digested it, and the corporal said:

'Aw-haw-hey. Think they're any good, sir?'

'Not as good as we are.'

'We're the wee boys,' said the corporal, and the wee boys
cried 'Way-ull,' mocking themselves. They were pleased at
the thought of another game, that was all. I doubt if their
reaction would have been different if their opponents had
been Moscow Dynamo or the Eye Infirmary.

The corporal and I pored over the team all morning; the
one doubtful spot was left-wing, and after much heart-
searching we fixed on McGlinchy, but the corporal didn't
like it. He at least knew what we were up against 'an' we
cannae afford a passenger. If Ah thought he'd wake up
mebbe half the match, OK, but no' kiddin', sir, yon yin's
no' a' there.'

'He's all we've got,' I said. 'Beattie's a half-back, and I'm
just not good enough. It's got to be McGlinchy.'

'Aye, weel,' said the corporal, 'that's so. But by half-time I'll bet we're wishin' we'd picked . . . McAuslan, even.'

In the unlikely event that we had been daft enough to do just that, we would have been disappointed. For when we embussed for the stadium McAuslan was mysteriously absent. We waited and swore, but he didn't appear, so Beattie was detailed to run the touchline, and off we went. With any luck McAuslan had fallen in the harbour.

The dressing-room was hot and sunny under the stand as we sat around waiting. The boys chewed gum and Mc-Glinchy played 'wee heidies' against the wall – nodding a ball against the partition like a boxer hitting a punch-ball. ('Close-mooth, tanner-ba' merchant,' muttered the corporal.) Outside we could hear the growing rumble of the crowd, and then there was the peep of a whistle, and the referee's step in the passage, and the boys shifted and said, 'Way-ull, way-ull,' and boots stamped and shorts were hitched, and outside a brass band was thumping out *Heart of Oak* and a great thunder of voices was rolling up as the Fleet came out, and the corporal sniffed and said :

'Awright, fellas, let's get stuck intae these matlows,' and I was left alone in the dressing-room.

I went out by the street door and was walking along to the grandstand entrance when I came face to face with Samuels in the crowd that was still pouring into the ground. It was a shock : I hadn't given him a thought since last night. Before I could say anything, he slapped me on the back, addressed me as Old Jocko, and said I was luv-ley.

'Goin' up to watch the slaughter?' he shouted. He was well ginned up. 'The massacre of the innocents, hey?'

'I like that,' I said. 'You've won enough off them; you could at least show some sympathy.'

'Who for?' he guffawed. 'The other lot?'

A horrible cold hand suddenly laid itself on the base of my spine.

'The other lot,' I said. 'You know who we're playing?'

'Been on the ship all mornin', checkin' stores,' he said, shaking his head. 'Who's the unfortunate party?'

'Tell me,' I said carefully. 'Have you put a bet on?'

'Have I, boyo? The lot, you bet. The sub-cheese. The bundle.'

I looked at my watch. It was two minutes to kick-off.

'Phone the bookie,' I said. 'Get it off. No matter what, cancel that bet.'

He didn't seem to be receiving me. 'The whole lot,' he said. 'Boyo, I cleaned out the safe. I shot the works. I'm tellin' . . .'

'Shut up, you Welsh oaf,' I shouted. 'Don't you understand? We're playing the Fleet, the Navy, all the great horrible battleships and aircraft carriers, millions of talented sailors. They will eat us alive. Your bet, if you let it ride, will go down the nick. Get it off.'

In all the world there is no sight so poignant as that of the confident mug when he feels the first sharp bite of the hook and realizes it is going to sink inexorably home. His face went from sweating red to dry grey, and he seemed to crumple.

'You're drunk, boyo,' he croaked.

'I'm drunk? Look who's talking. Look, Taffy, you'll have to cancel . . .' And just then what he had said came home to me. 'You say you cleaned out the safe? The ship's safe? But you've got two weeks of my Jocks' pay in there . . . Oh, brother.' I just stared at him. This was death, court-martial, ruin, and disaster. He was cooked. Unless the bet was scrubbed.

'It's no use,' he said. 'I cannot do it.' Odd, I thought, he says cannot, not can't. 'I didn't place it myself, see? The clerk did. Peterson. I gave him half a dozen addresses. I dunno where he is, now.'

The crowd was moving in, the last of it. There was nothing to be done. The band had stopped. I left him standing there, like a busted flush, and climbed the stairs to the stand. Poor Samuels, I thought. Idiot, mad Samuels. Of all the . . .

The roar hit me in the face as I came out into the stand.

I sat at the back of the main box; down front the Governor was starting work on his first handkerchief of the game, and beside him was a massive, grizzled hero in blue, with gold lace up to his armpits. That would be the Admiral. Their henchmen were about them, full of well-bred enthusiasm; the stadium was jammed, and every second man seemed to be a sailor. Our support was confined to a handful of khaki down below the box: our own reserves and a few associates.

'Flee-eet!' rolled across the brown, iron-hard pitch, and I saw the concentration of yellow shirts down near one goal: the Navy were attacking, powerful dark-blue figures with red stockings. They smacked the ball about with that tough assurance that is the mark of the professional; I saw the corporal slide in to tackle, and red stockings deftly side-stepped and swept the ball past him. The roar mounted, there was a surge in our goalmouth, and then the ball was trickling past into the crowd. I felt slightly sick.

'Get tore intae these people!' came from in front of the box, to be drowned in the Navy roar. Yes, I thought, get tore in. It's your pay and Samuels' reputation you're playing for. Then I thought, no, the heck with that, it's just for yourselves, that's all.

And they played. The hard ground and the light ball were on our side, for we were ball-players first and last; on grass the Navy would have been just too strong. They didn't rush things; they passed with deliberation and looked for their men, unlike our team, who were used to fast, short passing controlled by some sort of telepathy. If we played at their pace we were done for, so we didn't. The doll-like yellow figures moved and ran as though they were at practice, easy and confident.

We scored in the sixth minute, a zig-zag of passes down the middle that left Campbell, the centre, clear of the defence, and he lofted the ball over the Navy goalkeeper's head as he came out. There was a shocked roar from the crowd, a neigh of triumph from the Governor, a perceptible empurpling of the Admiral's neck, and an exulting 'Aw-haw-hey!' from below the box.

Two minutes later Campbell had the ball in the net again, but was ruled offside. Then he headed against the cross-bar, and we forced three corners in a row. But you could feel it slackening; the Fleet were as steady as ever, and presently they came away, swinging long passes through the open spaces, using their extra length of leg, keeping the ball up where their height counted. They *were* good; in their way. And for a moment, as they broke through on the left and centred and their inside right chose his spot in the net and banged in the equalizer, they were imposing that way.

There was worse to come. The Fleet went ahead with a penalty, when the corporal, in a momentary lapse into close-mouth warfare, obeyed our supporters' behest to 'Ca' the feet fae 'im,' and brought down a Navy forward close to goal. It was a critical point: when we kicked off again the Navy, one goal up, came storming through. Their centre got away and side-footed the ball past the advancing goal-keeper. It was rolling home, but the corporal came from nowhere and stopped it on the line. And then he did the ridiculous, unspeakable thing. I can still see him, the stocky yellow figure with his foot on top of the ball, watching three blue jerseys tearing down on him; alone, in his own goal. Bobby Moore himself would have belted it away for touch and been thankful. But not our boy. He shifted his hips, beat the first Navy forward on a sixpence, showed the ball to the other two, feinted amidst agonized yells of 'Get rid of it!' stepped over a scything foot, looked about him, and patted the ball into the hands of the goalkeeper, who was so stricken with anxiety that he nearly dropped it.

It was perhaps the cheekiest piece of ball-juggling that I've ever seen; it shook the Fleet momentarily for it seemed to indicate a careless contempt. It said, more clearly than words could have done, that there was no sense of panic in this defence. The Admiral roared with laughter, and I hoped again.

We scored again, just before the interval, a goal against the run of play headed in from a long, free kick, and the teams came off and the Marine band marched up and down playing *Iolanthe*. I stayed where I was, listening to the Governor chattering Good game, good game, my goodness, and the Admiral's bass rumble, and staring out at the sunlight on the great crowd lining the saucer of the arena. There was no point in my going down to the dressing-room; we were doing well, and nothing I could say could make it better.

The second half began disastrously. A high ball went into our goalmouth, the centre-half and the Fleet centre went up for it; the sailor came down on his feet and our man on his back. He lay still, and my heart turned over. I watched them lifting him, crowding around, but his head hung forward, and presently they took him behind the goal. 'Dirty, dirty!' came the cry from down front, drowned in the answering roar of 'Wheel 'im off!' from the Navy. The referee bounced the ball to restart the game, and as the injured man was supported towards the dressing-room I was bounding down the stairs.

He was slightly concussed, the doctor said; he wanted to go back on, but the doctor said it was out of the question. I watched while they bandaged his head, and told him – what I honestly felt – that it didn't matter a damn about the game. His face took on that look of whining rage that the Glaswegian wears in times of stress, and he said, 'We had them bate. We'd've sorted them this half.'

Maybe we would, I thought; with ten men it was certain that we wouldn't now. The doctor broke in to say that he ought to go to bed, and as they took him away I went back to the stand. Dimly I had been aware of the distant roar swelling and dying; when I climbed into my seat we were kicking off again. We were down 4–2.

The Fleet were out for blood now. Even the Admiral was joining in the roar, and the Governor was just sitting eating his hankie. Ten men don't look very different on the field from eleven; for a time they may even play above themselves, but they don't win. They never deserve to lose, but they lose.

Oddly enough, we held our own now, and with the tension gone I began to take in details. McClinchy was playing like an elderly horse; he hadn't seen much of the ball in the first half, and now he was using it as if it was a landmine, shying away from it, stumbling, and generally living up to the corporal's expectations. His inside man, little Forbes, was obviously cursing himself hoarse. The crowd enjoyed it.

'Windy!' roared the Fleet.

'Ah, you sharrap! Get back on the front o' the Players packet!'

'Turn blue, pongoes!'

'Play up,' cried the Governor. 'Come along, come along.'

The Admiral said something to him, and they both laughed, and I watched the handkerchief being twisted. There were about fifteen minutes left.

Then it happened, and you can read about it in the files of the Island's leading daily paper.

McClinchy got the ball and lost it; it came back to him and he fell over it and it went into touch. The Navy threw in, the ball ran to McGlinchy again, and for once he beat his man and was moving down the wing when a sailor whipped the heels from him. The crowd roared, McGlinchy got up hopping painfully, the Governor exclaimed, 'Oh, I say,' and little Forbes went scurrying in, fists clenched, to avenge the foul. Oh no, I said, please God, don't let Forbes hit him, not out there with everyone looking. Please don't, Forbes. But the referee was in between, shaking his finger, Forbes was hustled away by his mates, and the referee gave a free kick – against McGlinchy.

It was taken amid much hubbub, and I watched McGlinchy, standing looking puzzled, too surprised to protest, and then his head lifted, and the ball was running towards him. He stopped it, turned, swerved past the half-back, and was away. He could run when he wanted; he swerved in field, then out again towards the flag. The back went sliding in and McGlinchy side-stepped him and came in along the by-line, teasing that he was going to cross the ball, but holding it, like Matthews in his good years.

'Get rid of it!' cried an unhappy voice, but he held it, sand-dancing, looking up, and then he made a dart towards the near post, with the back straining at his heels, and he passed across and back when he couldn't have been more than three yards out, and Forbes had the empty goal in front of him.

The net shook, and the Admiral pounded his fist amidst the uproar, and the Governor made strange sounds, and I could see the corporal slapping McGlinchy's back and upbraiding him for holding on so long, and I thought regretfully that that had been McGlinchy's one brilliant flash. He was trotting back thoughtfully to his wing, with the applause dying down. It was 4–3 for the Navy and perhaps twelve minutes to go.

Then he did it again. Or very nearly. He went down the touch-line and then cut square across the field, beating two men on the way. He had an opening towards goal, with the Fleet defence floundering, but being McGlinchy he back-heeled the ball to nobody and it was cleared. I saw the corporal beating his breast, the Governor tore his handkerchief across, the Admiral bellowed jovially – and McGlinchy got the second chance he didn't deserve. The back's clearance hit a Fleet man and ran loose. McGlinchy, still in midfield, fastened on and this time went straight ahead, turned out to the left as the centre-half closed in, and centred hard and high. Duff, the right-winger, met it at the post with his head, and I realized that I was making ridiculous noises of triumph and delight. It was 4–4, the Fleet defence were gesturing at each other, and the little knot of yellow shirts was hurrying back towards the centre circle, embracing as they ran.

Then the Navy showed how good they were. They

attacked, and for the first time in my experience of them I saw my team panicked. They had snatched a possible draw from certain defeat, and they were scared stiff of slipping back. They were wild; they fouled twice, once perilously close to the eighteen-yard line, and I could see, although I couldn't hear, the corporal barking at them, swearing horribly, no doubt, steadying them. He was wise, that corporal; whenever he got the ball he looked for Mc-Glinchy. He sensed, like me, that he was in the presence of a phenomenon; it couldn't last, but he knew to use it while it was there. 'Feed him, feed him, he's bewitched,' I found myself saying, and McGlinchy went off down the wing, fair hair flying – I made a note to make him get it cut – and was tackled and the ball ran out.

He clapped his hands for it, trapped it as it was thrown in, back-heeled it through an opponent's legs, and ran on to it. He stopped, on the edge of the centre circle, foot on the ball, looking round. And for a split second the sound died. Then :

'Coom to 'im, man!' in a great Yorkshire voice.

'Get rid o' it, mac! See the winger.'

The roar swelled up, and he swerved away, dummied past a half-back, reached the penalty circle, slid heaven knows how between two defenders, almost lost the ball, scratched for it, flushed it forward, feinted to shoot, swerved again, and now he was on the penalty spot, with the blue jerseys converging, and little Forbes scream- ing for the ball, unmarked, and Campbell on the other side of him beating his hands. But he went on, the Admiral covered his face, the Governor rose to his feet cramming his handkerchief into his mouth, McGlinchy had one sailor at his elbow and another lunging desperately in front of him; he checked and side-stepped, looked at Forbes, shoved the ball under the tackler's leg, went after it, and just for a split second was clear, with every sailor except Lord Nelson thundering in on him, the goalkeeper diving at his feet, and then the blue flood swept down on him.

'Get rid o' it!'

'Kill him!' bawled the Admiral, decency forgotten.

'Get tore in!' cried the Governor.

He went down in a heap of navy jerseys, and a sudden bellow went up from behind the goal. I couldn't see why, and then I saw why. The ball was lying, rolling just a little, a foot over the goal-line. It came to rest in the net, just inside the post.

At such times, when all around is bedlam, the man of mark is distinguished by his nonchalance and detachment. Calmly I took out my cigarette case, selected a cigarette, struck a match, set fire to my sporran, roared aloud, dropped cigarettes, case, and matches, and scrambled on my knees along the floor of the box trying to beat the flames out. By the time I had succeeded the box was full of smoke and a most disgusting stench, one of the Admiral's aides was looking round muttering that expressions of triumph were all very well, but the line should be drawn somewhere, and the Fleet were kicking off in a last attempt to retrieve the game.

They didn't make it, but it was a near thing. There was one appeal for a penalty when the corporal seemed to handle – if I'd been the referee I believe I'd have given it – but the claim was disallowed, and then the long whistle blew. We had won, 5–4, and I found myself face to face with a red-faced petty officer who was exclaiming, 'By, you were lucky! I say, you were lucky! By!'

I made deprecating noises and shot downstairs. They were trooping into the dressing-room, chattering indignantly – it was their curious way not to be exultant over what had gone right, but aggrieved over what had gone wrong. I gathered that at least two of the Fleet should have been ordered off, that the referee had been ignorant of the offside law, that we should have had a penalty when . . . and so on. Never mind, I said, we won, it had all come out all right. Oh, aye, but . . .

The Governor looked in, beaming congratulation, and

there was a lot of noise and far too many people in the
dressing-room. The team were pulling off their jerseys and
trying to escape to the showers; clothes were falling on the
floor and bare feet were being stepped on; the Governor
was saying to Forbes, Well done, well played indeed, and
Forbes was saying See yon big, dirty, ignorant full-back,
and at last the door was shut and we were alone with the
smell of sweat and embrocation and steam and happy
weariness.

'Well done, kids,' I said, and the corporal said, 'No' sae
bad,' and rumpled McGlinchy's hair, and everyone laughed.
Through in the showers someone began to make mouth-
music to the tune of *The Black Bear*, and at the appropriate
moment the feet stamped in unison and the towel-clad
figures shuffled, clapping and humming.

'Not too loud,' I said. 'Don't let the Navy hear.'

I went over to McGlinchy, who was drying his hair and
whistling. I wanted to ask: What gets into you? Why
don't you play like that all the time? But I didn't. I knew
I wouldn't ever find out.

For no reason I suddenly thought of Samuels, and
realized that he was off the hook. Resentment quickly followed relief: he was not only in the clear, he had probably
made a small fortune. How lucky, how undeservedly lucky
can you get, I thought bitterly: but for McGlinchy's inexplicable brilliance Samuels would now be facing the certainty of court-martial and dismissal, possibly even prison.
As it was he was riding high.

Or so I thought until that evening, when I was summoned to the local bastille at the request of the Provost-
Marshal, to identify a soldier, one McAuslan, who had been
arrested during the afternoon. It appeared that he and an
anonymous sailor had been making a tour of all the bars in
town, and the sailor had eventually passed out in the street.
McAuslan's primitive efforts to minister to him had excited
attention, and the pair of them had been hauled off by the
redcaps.

They brought him out of his cell, looking abominable but apparently sober. I demanded to know what he thought he had been doing.

Well, it was like this, he and his friend the sailor had gone for a wee hauf, and then they had had anither, and . . .

'He'll be singing *I belong to Glasgow* in a minute,' observed the redcap corporal. 'Stand to attention, you thing, you.'

'Who was the sailor?' I asked, puzzled, for I remembered McAuslan's antipathy to the ship's crew.

'Wan o' the boys off the ship. Fella Peterson. He was gaun tae the toon, an' Ah offered tae staun' 'im a drink. Ye remember,' he went on earnestly, 'ye told me tae fraternize. Well, we fraternized, an' he got fu'. Awfy quick, he got fu',' McAuslan went on, and it was plain to see that his companion's incapacity offended him. 'He drank the drink Ah bought 'im, and it made 'im fleein', and then he was buyin' drink himsel' at an awfy rate . . .'

'That was the thing, sir,' explained the redcap. 'This sailor had more money than you've ever seen; he looked like he'd robbed a bank. That was really why we pulled them in, sir, for protection. Weedy little chap, the sailor, but he had hundreds of pounds worth of lire on him.'

Suddenly a great light dawned. Peterson was the name of Samuels' clerk, who had been going to place his bets for him, and McAuslan had obviously encountered him beforehand, and full of good fellowship had bought him liquor, and Peterson, the weedy little chap, must have been unused to strong waters, and had forgotten responsibility and duty and his captain's orders, and had proceeded to go on an almighty toot. So it seemed obvious that whatever custom the bookies had attracted that day, Samuels' had not been part of it. His money (and the ship's funds and my Jocks' pay) was safely in the military police office safe, less what McAuslan and Peterson had expended with crying 'Bring in!' Samuels could make that up himself, and serve him right. Also, he could have fun explaining to the MPs just how one of his sailors came to be rolling about town with all that cash on his person.

'McAuslan,' I said, 'in your own way you're a great man. Tell me,' I asked the redcap, 'are you going to charge him?'

'Well,' said the redcap, 'he wasn't what you'd call incapably stinking, just happy. It was the sailor who was paralytic. He still is. So . . .'

'Thank you,' I said. 'Look, McAuslan, you're a lucky man. You shouldn't go about getting little sailors stotius . . .'

'I was jist fraternizin', honest . . .'

'Right. You can fraternize some more. What I want you to do is go over to the ship, look out Lieutenant Samuels, and tell him, in your own well-chosen words, what happened today. Tell him the money's in the MP safe. And then you might offer to buy him a drink; he'll probably need one. And McAuslan, if he tries to hit you, you're not to clock him one, understand? Remember, be fraternal and polite; he's your superior officer and you wouldn't want to hurt his feelings.'

We took our leave of the civil redcaps, and I watched McAuslan striding purposefully towards the harbour, bonnet down over his eyes, to break the glad news to Samuels. It was growing dusk, and all in all, it had been quite a day.

I saw McGlinchy many years after, from the top of a Glasgow bus. Although his fair hair was fading and receding, and his face looked middle-aged and tired, there was no mistaking the loose-jointed, untidy walk. He was carrying a string bag, and he looked of no account at all in his stained raincoat and old shoes. And then the bus took me past. I wondered if he remembered those few minutes out in the sunlight. Perhaps not; he wasn't the kind who would think twice about it. But I remember McGlinchy when . . .

Wee Wullie

THE duties of a regimental orderly officer cover pretty well everything from inspecting the little iced cakes in the canteen to examining the prisoners in the guardroom cells to ensure that they are still breathing. In our battalion, the cells were seldom occupied; the discipline imposed on our volatile mixture of Aberdonians and Glaswegians was intelligent rather than tough, and more often than not trouble was dealt with before it got the length of a charge sheet.

So when I walked into the guardroom for a late-night look round and saw one of the cell doors closed and pad-locked, and a noise issuing from behind it like the honking of a drowsy seal, I asked McGarry, the provost sergeant, who his guest for the night might be.

'It's yon animal, Wee Wullie,' he said. 'Sharrap, ye Glas-gow heathen! He's gey fu', sir, an' half killed a redcap in the toon. They had to bring him here in a truck wi' his hands tied and a man sittin' on his heid. And afore I could get him in there I had to restrain him, mysel'.'

I realized that McGarry had a swelling bruise on one cheek and that his usually immaculate khaki shirt was crumpled; he was a big man, with forearms like a black-smith, and the skin on his knuckles was broken. I was glad it wasn't me he had had to restrain.

'He's sleepin' like a bairn noo, though,' he added, and he said it almost affectionately.

I looked through the grill of the cell. Wee Wullie was

lying on the plank, snoring like an organ. Between his mas-
sively booted feet at one end, and the bonnet on his grizzled
head at the other, there was about six and a half feet of
muscular development that would have done credit to a
mountain gorilla. One of his puttees was gone, his shirt
was in rags, and there was a tear in his kilt; his face, which
at the best of times was rugged, looked as though it had
been freshly trampled on. On the palm of one outstretched
hand still lay a trophy of his evening's entertainment – a
military police cap badge. In that enormous brown paw it
looked about as big as a sixpence.

'You did well to get him inside,' I told McGarry.

'Ach, he's no' bad tae manage when he's puggled,' said
the provost. 'A big, coorse loon, but the booze slows him
doon.'

I had some idea of what McGarry called 'no' bad tae
manage'. I recalled Hogmanay, when Wee Wullie had returned from some slight jollification in the Arab quarter
having whetted his appetite for battle on the local hostel-
ries, and erupted through the main gate intent on slaughter.
It had been at that moment of the day which, for a soldier,
is memorable above all others; the hour when the Last
Post is sounded, and everything else is still while the notes
float sadly away into the velvet dark; the guard stand stiffly
to attention by the main gate with the orderly officer behind, and the guardroom lanterns light up the odd little
ceremony that has hardly changed in essentials since the
Crimea. It is the end of the Army's day, peaceful and rather
beautiful.

Into this idyll had surged Wee Wullie, staggering drunk
and bawling for McGarry to come out and fight. For a
moment his voice had almost drowned the bugle, and then
(because he was Wee Wullie with thirty years' service
behind him) he had slowly come to attention and waited,
swaying like an oak in a storm, until the call was ended.
As the last note died away he hurled aside his bonnet,
reeled to the foot of the guardroom steps, and roared:

'Coom out, McGarry! Ah'm claimin' ye! Ye've had it, ye big Hielan' stirk! Ye neep! Ye teuchter, ye!'

McGarry came slowly out of the guardroom, nipping his cigarette, and calmly regarded the Neanderthal figure waiting for him. It looked only a matter of time before Wee Wullie started drumming on his chest and pulling down twigs to eat, but McGarry simply said,

'Aye, Wullie, ye're here again. Ye comin' quiet, boy?'

Wullie's reply was an inarticulate bellow and a furious fist-swinging charge, and five minutes later McGarry was kneeling over his prostrate form, patting his battered face, and summoning the guard to carry the body inside. They heaved the stricken giant up, and he came to himself just as they were manhandling him into the cooler. His blood-shot eyes rolled horribly and settled on McGarry, and he let out a great cry of baffled rage.

'Let me at 'im! Ah want at 'im!' He struggled furiously, and the four men of the guard clung to his limbs and wrestled him into the cell.

'Wheesht, Wullie,' said McGarry, locking the door. 'Just you lie doon like a good lad. Ye'll never learn; ye cannie fight McGarry when ye're fu'. Now just wheesht, or I'll come in tae ye.'

'You!' yelled Wullie through the bars. 'Oh, see you! Your mither's a Tory!'

McGarry laughed and left him to batter at the door until he was tired. It had become almost a ritual with the two of them, which would be concluded when Wullie had sobered up and told McGarry he was sorry. It was Wullie's enduring problem that he liked McGarry, and would fight with him only when inflamed by drink; yet drunk, he could not hope to beat him as he would have done sober.

I thought of these things as I looked into the cell at Wee Wullie asleep. On that wild Hogmanay I should, of course, have used my authority to reprimand and restrain him, and so prevented the unseemly brawl with the provost ser-geant, but you don't reprimand a rogue elephant or a snapped wire hawser, either of which would be as open to sweet reason as Wee Wullie with a bucket in him. The fact that he would have been overwhelmed by remorse afterwards for plastering me all over the guardroom wall would not really have been much consolation to either of us. So I had remained tactfully in the background while Sergeant McGarry had fulfilled his regimental duty of preserving order and repressing turbulence.

And now it had happened again, for the umpteenth time, but this time it was bad. From what McGarry had told me, Wee Wullie had laid violent hands on a military policeman, which meant that he might well be court-martialled – which, inevitably, for a man with a record like his, would mean a long stretch in the glasshouse at Cairo.

'He'll no' get away wi' it this time, poor loon,' said McGarry. 'It'll be outwith the battalion, ye see Aye, auld Wullie, he'll be the forgotten man of Heliopolis nick if the redcaps get their way.' He added, apparently irrelevantly, 'For a' the Colonel can say.'

I left the guardroom and walked across the starlit parade ground through the grove of tamarisks to the white-walled subalterns' quarters, wondering if this was really the finish of Wee Wullie. If it was, well, the obvious thing to do would be to thank God we were rid of a knave, an even bigger battalion pest than the famous Private McAuslan, the dirtiest soldier in the world, an Ishmael, a menace, a horrible man. At the same time . . .

All that was really wrong with Wee Wullie was his predilection for strong drink and violent trouble. He was drunk the first time I ever saw him, on a desert convoy passing under Marble Arch, that towering monument to Mussolini's vanity which bestrides the road on the Libyan border. I had noticed this huge man, first for his very size, secondly for his resemblance to the late William Bendix, and lastly for his condition, which was scandalous. He was patently tight, but still at the good-humoured stage, and was being helped aboard a truck by half a dozen well-wishers. They dropped him several times, and he lay in the sand roaring. I was a green subaltern, but just experienced enough to know when not to intervene, so I left them to it, and eventually they got him over the tailboard. (It is astonishing just how often an officer's duty seems to consist of looking the other way, or maybe I was just a bad officer.)

In the battalion itself he was a curious mixture. As far as the small change of soldiering went, Wullie was reasonably efficient. His kit at inspections was faultless, his knowledge and deportment exact, so far as they went, which was just far enough for competence. In his early days he had been as high as sergeant before being busted (I once asked the adjutant when this had been, and he said, 'God knows, about the first Afghan War, I should think'), but in later years the authorities had despaired of promoting him to any rank consistent with his length of service. Occasionally they would make him a lance-corporal, just for variety, and then Wullie would pick a fight with the American Marines, or tip a truck over, or fall in alcoholic stupor into a river and have to be rescued, and off would come his stripe again. He had actual Service chevrons literally as long as his arm, but badges of rank and good conduct he had none.

Yet he enjoyed a curiously privileged position. In drill, for example, it was understood that there were three ways of doing things: the right way, the wrong way, and Wee Wullie's way. His movements were that much slower, more ponderous, than anyone else's; when he saluted, his hand did not come up in a flashing arc, but jerked up so far, and then travelled slowly to his right eyebrow. On parade, there was some incongruity in the sight of a platoon of wee Gleska keelies and great-chested Aberdonians (who run to no spectacular height, as a rule) with Gargantua in their midst, his rifle like a popgun in his huge fist, and himself going through the motions with tremendous intensity, half a second behind everyone else. There was almost a challenge in the way he performed, as though he was conscious of being different, and yet there was about him a great dignity. Even the Regimental Sergeant Major recognized it, and excused much.

This was when he was sober and passive. Even then he was withdrawn and monosyllabic; only when he was slightly inebriated could he be described as sociable. Beyond that he was just outrageous, a dangerous, wickedly powerful ruffian whom only the redoubtable McGarry could manage single-handed.

Yet there was in the battalion a curiously protective instinct towards him. It seemed to emanate from the Colonel, who had ordered that Wullie was never to be brought before him for disciplinary action except when it was unavoidable. Thus his crimes and misdemeanours were usually dealt with at company level, and he got off fairly lightly. When the Colonel did have to deal with him he would consign Wullie to the cells and afterwards try to find him a quiet niche where he would be out of trouble, invariably without success. When he was made medical orderly he got at the MO's medicinal brandy and wrecked the place; he lost the job of padre's batman through his unceasing profanity; attached to the motor-transport section he got tremendously high and put a three-ton truck through a brick wall ('I always said that particular experiment was sheer lunacy,' said the adjutant. 'I mean, a truck was all he needed, wasn't it?'). An attempt was even made to get him into the band, and the little pipe-sergeant was scandalized. 'He has no sense of time, Colonel, sir,' he protested. 'Forbye, look at the size of his feet, and think of that clumph-clumph-clumphing on the great ceremonial parades.'

In the end he was made the MO's gardener, and he seemed to take to it. He did not do any actual gardening himself, but he could address the Arab gardeners in their own language, and got all the plants neatly arranged in columns of threes, dressed by the right, and in order of what he considered their seniority. For in his quiet moments there was a strong military sense in Wullie, as there should have been after thirty years in uniform. This was brought home to me in the only conversation of any duration I ever had with him, one day when I was orderly officer and was inspecting the whitewashed stones which Wullie's Arabs were arranging in the headquarters plot. For some reason I mentioned to Wullie that I was not intending to stay in the Army when my number came up, and he said, with his direct, intent stare, 'Then ye're a fool, sir.' Only Wullie could have called an officer a fool, in a way which carried no disrespect, and only Wullie would have added 'sir' to the rebuke.

And on another occasion he did me a great service. It was shortly after his Hogmanay escapade, and I was again orderly officer and was supervising the closing of the wet canteen. The joint was jumping and I hammered with my walking-stick on the bar and shouted, 'Last drinks. Time, gentleman, please,' which was always good for a laugh. Most of them drank and went, but there was one bunch, East End Glaswegians with their bonnets pulled down over their eyes, who stayed at their table. Each man had about three pints in front of him; they had been stocking up.

'Come on,' I said. 'Get it down you.'

There were a few covert grins, and someone muttered about being entitled to finish their drinks – which strictly speaking they were. But there was no question they were trying it on : on the other hand, how does a subaltern move men who don't want to be moved? I know, personality. Try it some time along the Springfield Road.

'You've got two minutes,' I said, and went to supervise the closing of the bar shutters. Two minutes later I looked across; they were still there, having a laugh and taking their time.

I hesitated; this was one of those moments when you can look very silly, or lose your reputation, or both. At that moment Wee Wullie, who had been finishing his pint in a corner, walked past and stopped to adjust his bonnet near me.

'Tak' wan o' them by the scruff o' the neck and heave 'im oot,' he said, staring at me, and then went out of the canteen.

It was astonishing advice. About the most awful crime an officer can commit is to lay hands on an other rank. Suppose one of them belted me? It could be one hell of a mess, and a scandal. Then one of them laughed again, loudly, and I strode across to the table, took the nearest man (the smallest one, incidentally) by the collar, and hauled him bodily to the door. He was too surprised to do anything; he was off balance all the way until I dropped him just outside the doorway.

He was coming up, spitting oaths and murder, when Wee Wullie said out of the shadows at one side of the door:

'Jist you stay down, boy, or ye'll stay down for the night.'

I went into the canteen again. The rest were standing, staring. 'Out,' I said, like Burt Lancaster in the movies, and they went, leaving their pints. When I left the canteen Wee Wullie had disappeared.

And now he was probably going to disappear for keeps, I thought that night after seeing him in the cell. How long would he get for assaulting a redcap? Two years? How old was he, and how would he last out two years on the hill, or the wells, or whatever diversions they were using now in the glasshouse? Of course, he was as strong as an ox. And what had McGarry meant, 'For a' the Colonel can say'?

What the Colonel did say emerged a few days later when the adjutant, entering like Rumour painted full of tongues, recounted what had taken place at Battalion HQ when the town Provost Marshal had called. The PM had observed that the time had come when Wee Wullie could finally get his come-uppance, and had spoken of general courts-martial and long terms of detention. The Colonel had said, uh-huh, indeed, and suggested that so much was hardly necessary: it could be dealt with inside the battalion. By no means, said the PM, Wee Wullie had been an offence to the public weal too long; he was glasshouse-ripe; a turbulent, ungodly person whom he, the PM, was going to see sent where he wouldn't hear the dogs bark. The Colonel then asked, quietly, if the PM, as a special favour to him, would leave the matter entirely in the Colonel's hands.

Taken aback, the PM protested at length, and whenever he paused for breath the Colonel would raise his great bald hawk head and gently repeat his request. This endured for about twenty minutes, after which the PM gave way under protest – under strong protest – and stumped off muttering about protecting pariahs and giving Capone a pound out of the poor box. He was an angry and bewildered man.

'So the matter need not go to the General Officer Commanding,' concluded the adjutant mysteriously. 'This time.' Pressed for details, he explained, in a tone that suggested he didn't quite believe it himself, that the Colonel had been ready, if the PM had been obdurate, to go to the GOC on Wee Wullie's behalf.

'All the way, mark you,' said the adjutant. 'For that big idiot. Of course, if the GOC happens to have been your fag at Rugby, I dare say it makes it easier, but I still don't understand it.'

Nor did anyone else. Generals were big stuff, and Wullie was only one extremely bad hat of a private. The Colonel called him several other names as well, when the case came up at orderly room, and gave him twenty-eight days, which was as much as he could award him without sending him to the military prison.

So Wullie did his time in the battalion cells, expressing repentance while he cleaned out the ablutions, and exactly twenty-four hours after his release he was back inside for drunkenness, insubordination, and assault, in that he, in the cookhouse, did wilfully overturn a cauldron of soup and, on being reprimanded by the cook-sergeant, did strike the cook-sergeant with his fist . . .

And so on. 'I don't know,' said the adjutant in despair. 'Short of shooting him, what *can* you do with him? What *can* you do?'

He asked the question at dinner, in the Colonel's absence. It was not a mess night, and we were eating our spam informally. Most of the senior officers were out in their married quarters; only the second-in-command, a grizzled major who was also a bachelor, represented the old brigade. He sat chewing his cheroot absently while the adjutant went on to say that it couldn't last for ever; the Colonel's curious – and misguided – protection of Wee Wullie would have to stop eventually. And when it did, Wee Wullie would be away, permanently.

The second-in-command took out his cheroot and inspected it. 'Well, it won't stop, I can tell you that,' he said.

The adjutant demanded to know why, and the second-in-command explained.

'Wee Wullie may get his deserts one of these days; it's a matter of luck. But I do know that it will be over the Colonel's dead body. You expressed surprise that the Colonel would go to the GOC; I'm perfectly certain he would go farther than that if he had to.'

'For Heaven's sake, why? What's so special about Wee Wullie?'

'Well, he and the Colonel have served together a long time. Since the first war, in fact. Same battalion, war and peace, for most of the time – joined almost the same day, I believe. Wounded together at Passchendaele, that sort of thing.'

'We all know that,' said the adjutant impatiently. 'But even so, granted the Colonel feels responsible, I'd have said Wee Wullie has overstepped the mark too far and too often. He's a dead loss.'

'Well,' said the second-in-command, 'that's as may be.' He sat for a moment rolling a new cheroot in his fingers. 'But there are things you don't know.' He lit the cheroot and took a big breath. Everyone was listening and watching.

'You know,' said the second-in-command, 'that after the battalion came out of France in 'forty, it was sent to the Far East. Well, Wullie didn't go with it. He was doing time in Sowerby Bridge glasshouse, for the usual offences — drunkenness, assault on a superior, and so on. When he came out the battalion had gone into the bag after Singapore, so Wullie was posted to one of our Terrier battalions in North Africa — it was Tom Crawford's, in fact. I don't suppose Tom was particularly happy to see the regiment's Public Enemy Number One, but he had other things to think about. It was the time when the desert war was going to and fro like ping-pong — first Rommel on top, then us — and his battalion had taken a pretty fair hammering, one way and another.

'Anyway, when Rommel made his big breakthrough, and looked like going all the way to Shepheard's Hotel, Tom's chaps were being pushed back with the rest. There was some messy fighting, and in it they picked up a prisoner — a warrant officer in the German equivalent of the service corps. They learned from him about the existence of one of those petrol dumps that Rommel had put down on an earlier push — you know the sort of thing, we did it, too. When you're on the run you bury all the fuel you can, and when you come back that way, there it is. How they got this chap to spill the beans I don't know, but he did.

'Well, Tom saw at once that if they could scupper this buried dump it might be a telling blow to the Jerry advance, so he went after it. One of his company commanders, fellow called MacLennan, took off with a truck, a couple of Sappers, the German prisoner as a guide, a driver — and Wee Wullie. They took him along because he was big and rough, and just the chap to keep an eye on the Hun. And off they went into the blue to blow the dump sky-high.

'It was away out of the main run, down to the southward, and it was going to be a near thing for them to get there before Rommel's crowd, so they went hell for leather. They didn't make it. Somewhere along the way the truck went over a land-mine, the driver was killed, and Mac-Lennan's knee-cap was smashed. The Sappers and Wullie and the Hun were just shaken, but the truck was a complete write-off. And there they were, miles behind their own retreating brigade, stranded in the middle of God knows where, and no way of getting home but walking.'

The second-in-command's cheroot had gone out. He chewed it out of the side of his mouth, staring at the tablecloth.

'You know what the desert's like. If you haven't got transport, you die. Unless someone finds you. And Mac-Lennan knew the only people who might find them were the Germans, and that was a thin chance at best. If they'd made it to the dump it would have been different. As it was, they would have to shift for themselves – with about two days' water and upwards of forty miles to go before they had even a reasonable chance of being picked up.

'McLennan couldn't go, of course, with his leg smashed. He got them to make him comfortable in the lee of the wrecked truck, kept one water bottle himself, and ordered the four of them to clear out. One of the Sappers wanted to stay with him, but MacLennan knew there was no point to it. Barring miracles, he was done for. He just laid down the law to them, told them to head north, and wished them luck. Wee Wullie never said anything, apparently – not that that was unusual, since he was sober.

'MacLennan watched them set off, into that hellish burning waste, and then settled down to die. He supposed his water might last him through the next day, and decided that whatever happened, he wouldn't shoot himself. Cool boy, that one. He's at Staff College now, I believe. But it didn't come to that; his miracle happened. Up north, although he didn't know it, Rommel was just coming to a halt near Alamein, and by sheer chance on the second day one of our long-range group patrols came on him just as he was drinking the last of his water.'

The second-in-command paused to relight his cheroot, and I noticed the adjutant's hand stray towards his glass, and stop halfway.

'Well, they took MacLennan in,' said the second-in-command, 'and of course he got them on the hunt right away for the other four. It took them some time. They found one body about twenty miles north of where Mac-Lennan had been, and another a little farther on. And when they were on the point of giving up, they found Wee Wullie. He was walking north, or rather, he was staggering north, and he was carrying the fourth chap in a fireman's lift.

'He was in a fearful state. His face was black, his tongue and mouth were horribly dried up, all his gear was gone, of course, and he must have been on the very edge of collapse. He couldn't see, he couldn't hear, he couldn't speak – but he could march. God knows how long he'd been without water, or how long he'd been carrying the other fellow; he was so done that when they found him they had to stop him, physically, in his tracks, because they couldn't make him understand. One of them said afterwards' – the second-in-command hesitated and drew on his cheroot – 'that he believed Wee Wullie would just have gone on for ever.'

Knowing Wee Wullie, I could have believed it too. After a moment the adjutant said : 'That was pretty good. Didn't he – well, he hasn't any decorations, has he? You'd have thought, seeing he saved a comrade's life—'

'It wasn't a comrade,' said the second-in-comand. 'He was carrying the German. And it didn't save his life. He died soon after.'

'Even so,' said the adjutant. 'It was pretty bloody heroic.'

'I'd say so,' said the second-in-command. 'But Wee Wullie's his own worst enemy. When he was taken back to base and the hospital, he made a splendid recovery. Managed to get hold of drink, somehow, terrified the nursing staff, climbed out on the roof and sang *The Ball* of *Kirrie-muir* at the top of his voice—all seventy-odd verses, they tell me. They tried to drag him in, and he broke a military police-man's jaw. Then he fell off the roof and got concusson. It isn't easy to hang gongs on a man like that. Although I dare say if it had been, say, MacLennan that he'd been carrying, and not the German, that might have made a difference.'

'Well,' said the adjutant, 'it would have made our Colonel's attitude . . . well, easier to understand.'

'Maybe that's the point,' said the second-in-command. 'Wee Wullie tried to save an enemy. The German to him was really a nuisance – a dead loss. But he was prepared to risk his own life for him, to go all the way. I don't know. Anyway,' he added, looking as near embarrassment as was possible for him, 'that may explain some of the things you haven't understood about him. Why, as far as the Colonel is concerned, he can set fire to the barracks and murder half the redcaps in the garrison, but the Colonel will still be bound to go all along the line for him. So will I, if it means the GOC, and the High Command, the whole lot. And so will the battalion. It's an odd situation. Oh, perhaps Wullie understands it and plays on it. So what? I know the Provost-Marshal's right: he's a drunken, dangerous dis-graceful, useless ruffian. But whenever I see him at his worst, I can't help thinking of him going through that desert, marching, and not falling. Just marching. Now, where's the ludo set? There isn't a subaltern can live with me on the board tonight.'

I have my own view of Wee Wullie, which is naturally coloured by my own experience of him. When I finally left the battalion, he was still there, pottering about the MO's garden and fighting with the guard; they were still protect-ing him, rightly or wrongly. What is worth protecting? Anyway, his story is as I saw it, and as the second-in-command told it to me. Only the times have changed.

The General Danced at Dawn

FRIDAY night was always dancing night. On the six other evenings of the week the officers' mess was informal, and we had supper in various states of uniform, mufti and undress, throwing bits of bread across the table and invading the kitchen for second helpings of caramel pudding. The veranda was always open, and the soft, dark night of North Africa hung around pleasantly beyond the screens.

Afterwards in the anteroom we played cards, or ludo, or occasional games of touch rugby, or just talked the kind of nonsense that subalterns talk, and whichever of these things we did our seniors either joined in or ignored completely; I have seen a game of touch rugby in progress, with the chairs and tables pushed back against the wall, and a heaving mass of Young Scotland wrestling for a 'ball' made of sock stuffed with rags, while less than a yard away the adjutant, two company commanders, and the MO were sitting round a card table holding an inquest on five spades doubled. There was great toleration.

Friday night was different. On that evening we dressed in our best tartans and walked over to the mess in twos and threes as soon as the solitary piper, who had been playing outside the mess for about twenty minutes broke into the slow, plaintive *Battle of the Somme* – or, as it is known colloquially, 'See's the key, or I'll roar up yer lobby.'

In the mess we would have a drink in the anteroom, the captains and the majors sniffing at their Talisker and Glen-grant, and the rest of us having beer or orange juice – I have known messes where subalterns felt they had to drink hard stuff for fear of being thought cissies, but in a Highland mess nobody presses anybody. For one thing, no senior officer with a whisky throat wants to see his single malt being wasted on some pink and eager one-pipper.

Presently the Colonel would knock his pipe out and limp into the dining-room, and we would follow in to sit round the huge white table. I never saw a table like it, and never expect to; Lord Mayors banquets, college dinners, and American conventions at a hundred dollars a plate may surpass it in spectacular grandeur, but when you sat down at this table you were conscious of sitting at a dinner that had lasted for centuries.

The table was a mass of silver: the horse's-hoof snuff-box that was a relic of the few minutes at Waterloo when the regiment broke Napoleon's cavalry, and Wellington himself took off his hat and said, 'Thank you, gentlemen'; the set of spoons from some forgotten Indian palace with strange gods carved on the handles; the great bowl, magnificently engraved, presented by an American infantry regiment in Normandy, and the little quaich that had been found in the dust at Magersfontein; loot that had come from Vienna, Moscow, Berlin, Rome, the Taku Forts, and God knows where, some direct and some via French, Prussian, Polish, Spanish, and other regiments from half the countries on earth – stolen, presented, captured, bought, won, given, taken, and acquired by accident. It was priceless, and as you sat and contemplated it you could almost feel the shades elbowing you round the table.

At any rate, it enabled us to get through the tinned tomato soup, rissoles and jam tart, which seemed barely adequate to such a splendid setting, or to the sonorous grace which the padre had said beforehand ("I say, padre, can you say it in Gaelic?' 'Away, a' he talks is Glesca.' 'Wheesht for the minister'). And when it was done and the youth who was vice-president had said, 'The King,' passed the port in the wrong direction, giggled, upset his glass, and been sorrowfully rebuked from the table head, we lit up and waited for the piper. The voices, English of Sandhurst and Scottish of Kelvinside, Perthshire, and Peterhead, died away, and the pipe-major strode in and let us have it.

A twenty-minute pibroch is no small thing at a range of four feet. Some liked it, some affected to like it, and some buried their heads in their hands and endured it. But in everyone the harsh, keening siren-sound at least provoked thought. I can see them still, the faces round the table; the sad padre, tapping slowly to *The Battle of the Spoiled Dyke;* the junior subaltern, with his mouth slightly open, watching the tobacco smoke wreathing in low clouds over the white cloth; the signals officer, tapping his thumb-nail against his teeth and shifting restlessly as he wondered if he would get away in time to meet that Ensa singer at the club; the Colonel, chin on fist like a great bald eagle with his pipe clamped between his teeth and his eyes two generations away; the men, the boys, the dreamer's eyes and the boozer's melancholy, all silent while the music enveloped them.

When it was over, and we had thumped the table, and the pipe-major had downed his whisky with a Gaelic toast, we would troop out again, and the Colonel would grin and rub tobacco between his palms, and say :

'Right, gentlemen, shall we dance?'

This was part of the weekly ritual. We would take off our tunics, and the pipers would make preparatory whines, and the Colonel would perch on a table, swinging his game leg which the Japanese had broken for him on the railway, and would say :

'Now, gentlemen, as you know there is Highland dancing as performed when ladies are present, and there is Highland dancing. We will have Highland dancing. In Valetta in '21 I saw a Strip the Willow performed in eighty-nine seconds, and an Eightsome reel in two minutes twenty-two seconds. These are our targets. All right, pipey.'

We lined up and went at it. You probably know both the dances referred to, but until you have seen Highland subalterns and captains giving them the treatment you just don't appreciate them. Strip the Willow at speed is lethal; there is much swinging round, and when fifteen stone of heughing humanity is whirled at you at close range you have to be wide awake to sidestep, scoop him in, and hurl him back again. I have gone up the line many times, and it is like being bounced from wall to wall of a long corridor with heavy weights attached to your arms. You just have to relax and concentrate on keeping upright.

Occasionally there would be an accident, as when the padre, his Hebridean paganism surging up through his Calvinistic crust, swung into the MO, and the latter, his constitution undermined by drink and peering through microscopes, mistimed him and received him heavily amidships. The padre simply cried: 'The sword of the Lord and of Gideon!' and danced on, but the MO had to be carried to the rear and his place taken by the second-in-command, who was six feet four and a danger in traffic.

The Eightsome was even faster, but not so hazardous, and when it was over we would have a breather while the adjutant, a lanky Englishman who was transformed by pipe music into a kind of Fred Astaire, danced a 'ragged trousers' and the cooks and mess waiters came through to watch and join in the gradually mounting rumble of stamping and applause. He was the clumsiest creature in everyday walking and moving, but out there, with his fair hair falling over his face and his shirt hanging open, he was like thistledown on the air; he could have left Nijinsky frozen against the cushion.

The pipe-sergeant loved him, and the pipe-sergeant had skipped nimbly off with prizes uncounted at gatherings and games all over Scotland. He was a tiny, indiarubber man, one of your technically perfect dancers who had performed before crowned heads, viceroys, ambassadors, 'and all sorts of wog presidents and the like of that'. It was to mollify

him that the Colonel would encourage the adjutant to perform, for the pipe-sergeant disliked 'wild' dancing of the
Strip the Willow variety, and while we were on the floor he
would stand with his mouth primly pursed and his glen-
garry pulled down, glancing occasionally at the Colonel and
sniffing.

'What's up, pipe-sarnt,' the Colonel would say, 'too slow
for you?'

'Slow?' the pipe-sergeant would say. 'Fine you know, sir,
it's not too slow for me. It's a godless stramash is what it is,
and shouldn't be allowed. Look at the unfortunate Mr
Cameron, the condition of him; he doesn't know whether
it's Tuesday or breakfast.'

'They love it; anyway, you don't want them dancing like
a bunch of old women.'

'No, not like old women, but chust like proper Highland-
men. There is a form, and a time, and a one-two-three, and
a one-two-three, and, thank God, it's done and here's the
lovely adjutant.'

'Well, don't worry,' said the Colonel, clapping him on
the shoulder. 'You get 'em twice a week in the mornings to
show them how it ought to be done.'

This was so. On Tuesdays and Thursdays batmen would
rouse officers with malicious satisfaction at 5.30, and we
would stumble down, bleary and unshaven, to the MT
sheds, where the pipe-sergeant would be waiting, skipping in
the cold to put us through our session of practice dancing.
He was in his element, bounding about in his laced pumps,
squeaking at us while the piper played and we galumphed
through our eightsomes and foursomes. Unlovely we were,
but the pipe-sergeant was lost in the music and the mists of
time, emerging from time to time to rebuke, encourage and
commend.

'Ah, the fine sound,' he would cry, pirouetting among us.
'And a one, two, three, and a one, two, three. And there we
are, Captain MacAlpine, going grand, going capital! One,
two, three and oh, observe the fine feet of Captain Mac-

Alpine! He springs like a startled ewe, he does! And a one, two, three, Mr Elphinstone-Hamilton, and a pas-de-bas, and, yes, Mr Cameron, once again. But now a one, two, three, four, Mr Cameron, and a one, two, three, four, and the rocking-step. Come to me, Mr Cameron, like a full-rigged ship. But, oh, dear God, the horns of the deer! Boldly, proudly, that's the style of the masterful Mr Cameron; his caber feidh is wonderful, it is fit to frighten Napoleon.'

He and Ninette de Valois would have got on a fair treat. The Colonel would sometimes loaf down, with his great-coat over his pyjamas, and lean on his cromach, smoking and smiling quietly. And the pipe-sergeant, carried away, would skip all the harder and direct his running commentary at his audience of one.

'And a one, two, three, good morning to you, sir, see the fine dancing, and especially of Captain MacAlpine! One, two, three, and a wee bit more, Mr Cameron, see the fine horns of the deer, Colonel sir, how he knacks his thoos, God bless him. Ah, yes, that is it, Mr Elphinstone-Hamilton, a most proper appearance, is it not, Colonel?'

'I used to think,' the Colonel would say later, 'that the pipe-sergeant must drink steadily from three AM to get into that elevated condition. Now I know better. The man's be-witched.'

So we danced, and it was just part of garrison life, until the word came of one of our periodic inspections, which meant that a general would descend from Cairo and storm through us, and report to GHQ on our condition, and the Colonel, Adjutant, Regimental Sergeant Major and so on would either receive respective rockets or pats on the back. Especially the Colonel. And this inspection was rather more than ordinarily important to the old boy, because in two months he and the battalion would be going home, and soon after that he would be retiring. He should by rights have retired long before, but the war had kept him on, and he had stayed to the last possible minute. After all it was his life: he had gone with this battalion to France in '14 and hardly left it since; now he was going for good, and the word went round that his last inspection on active service must be something for him to remember in his old age, when he could look back on a battalion so perfect that the inspecting general had not been able to find so much as a speck of whitewash out of place. So we hoped.

Now, it chanced that, possibly in deference to the Colonel, the very senior officer who made this inspection was also very Highland. The pipe-sergeant rubbed his hands at the news. 'There will be dancing,' he said, with the air of the Creator establishing land and sea. 'General MacCrimmon will be enchanted; he was in the Argylls, where they dance a wee bit. Of course, being an Argyll he is chust a kind of Campbell, but it will have to be right dancing for him, I can assure you, one, two, three, and no lascivious jiving.'

Bursting with zeal, he worked our junior officers' dancing class harder than ever, leaping and exhorting until he had us exhausted; meanwhile, the whole barracks was humming with increased activity as we prepared for inspection. Arab sweepers brushed the parade ground with hand brushes to free it of dust, whitewash squads were everywhere with their buckets and stained overalls; every weapon in the place, from dirks and revolvers to the three-inch mortars, was stripped and oiled and cleaned three times over; the cookhouses, transport sheds, and even the little church, were meticulously gone over; Private McAuslan, the dirtiest soldier in the world, was sent on leave, squads roamed the barrack grounds continually, picking up paper, twigs, leaves, stones, and anything that might offend the military symmetry; the Colonel snapped and twisted his handkerchief and broke his favourite pipe; sergeants became hoarse and fretful, corporals fearful, and the quartermasters and company clerks moved uneasily in the dark places of their stores, sweating in the knowledge of duty ill-done and judgement at hand. But, finally, we were ready; in other words we were clean. We were so tired that we couldn't have withstood an attack by the Tiller Girls, but we were clean.

The day came, and disaster struck immediately. The sentry at the main gate turned out the guard at the approach of the General's car, and dropped his rifle in presenting arms. That was fairly trivial, but the General commented on it as he stepped out to be welcomed by the Colonel, and that put everyone's nerves on edge; matters were not improved by the obvious fact that he was pleased to have found a fault so early, and was intent on finding more.

He didn't have far to look. He was a big, beefy man, turned out in a yellowing balmoral and an ancient, but beautifully cut kilt, and his aide was seven feet of sideways invisibility in one of the Guards regiments. The General announced that he would begin with the men's canteen ('men's welfare comes first with me; should come first with every officer'), and in the panic that ensued on this unexpected move the canteen staff upset a swill-tub in the middle of the floor five seconds before he arrived; it had been a fine swill-tub, specially prepared to show that we had such things, and he shouldn't have seen it until it had been placed at a proper distance from the premises.

The General looked at the mess, said 'Mmh,' and asked to see the medical room ('always assuming it isn't rife with bubonic plague'); it wasn't, as it happened, but the MO's terrier had chosen that morning to give birth to puppies, beating the adjutant to it by a short head. Thereafter a fire broke out in the cookhouse, a bren-gun carrier broke down, an empty cigarette packet was found in 'B' Company's garden, and Private McAuslan came back off leave. He was tastefully dressed in shirt and boots, but no kilt, and entered the main gate in the company of three military policemen who had foolishly rescued him from a canal into which he had fallen. The General noted his progress to the guardroom with interest; McAuslan was alternately singing the Twenty-third Psalm and threatening to write to his Member of Parliament.

So it went on; anything that could go wrong, seemed to go wrong, and by dinner-time that night the General was wearing a sour and satisfied expression, his aide was silently contemptuous, the battalion was boiling with frustration and resentment, and the Colonel was looking old and ill. Only once did he show a flash of spirit, and that was when the junior subaltern passed the port the wrong way again, and the General sighed, and the Colonel caught the subaltern's eye and said loudly and clearly: 'Don't worry, Ian; it doesn't matter a damn.'

That finally froze the evening over, so to speak, and when we were all back in the anteroom and the senior major remarked that the pipe-sergeant was all set for the dancing to begin, the Colonel barely nodded, and the General lit a cigar and sat back with the air of one who was only mildly interested to see how big a hash we could make of this too.

Oddly enough, we didn't. We danced very well, with the pipe-sergeant fidgeting on the outskirts, hoarsely whispering, 'One, two, three,' and afterwards he and the adjutant and two of the best subalterns danced a foursome that would have swept the decks at Braemar. It was good stuff, really good, and the General must have known it, but he seemed rather irritated than pleased. He kept moving in his seat, frowning, and when we had danced an eightsome he finally turned to the Colonel.

'Yes, it's all right,' he said. 'But, you know, I never cared much for the set stuff. Did you never dance a sixteensome?'

The Colonel said he had heard of such a thing, but had not, personally, danced it.

'Quite simple,' said the General, rising. 'Now, then. Eight more officers on the floor. I think I remember it, although it's years now . . .'

He did remember; a sixteensome is complicated, but its execution gives you the satisfaction that you get from any complex manoeuvre; we danced it twice, the General calling the changes and clapping (his aide was studying the ceiling with the air of an archbishop at a cannibal feast), and when it was over the General actually smiled and called for a large whisky. He then summoned the pipe-sergeant, who was looking disapproving.

'Pipe-sergeant, tell you what,' said the General. 'I have been told that back in the Nineties the First Black Watch sergeants danced a thirty-twosome. Always doubted it, but suppose it's possible. What do you think? Yes, another whisky, please.'

The pipe-sergeant, flattered but slightly outraged, gave his opinion. All things were possible; right, said the General, wiping his mouth, we would try it.

The convolutions of an eightsome are fairly simple; those of a sixteensome are difficult, but a thirty-twosome is just murder. When you have thirty-two people weaving and circling it is necessary that each one should move precisely right, and that takes organization. The General was an organizer; his tunic came off after half an hour, and his voice hoarsely thundered the time and the changes. The mess shook to the crash of feet and the skirling of the pipes, and at last the thirty-twosome rumbled, successfully, to its ponderous close.

'Dam' good! Dam' good!' exclaimed the General, flushed and applauding. 'Well danced, gen'men. Good show, pipe-sarn't! Thanks, Tom, don't mind if I do. Dam' fine dancing. Thirty-twosome, eh? That'll show the Black Watch!'

He seemed to sway a little as he put down his glass. It was midnight, but he was plainly waking up.

'Thirty-twosome, by Jove! Wouldn't have thought it possible.' A thought seemed to strike him. 'I say, pipe-sarn't, I wonder ... d'you suppose that's as far as we can go? I mean is there any reason? ...'

He talked, and the pipe-sergeant's eyes bulged. He shook his head, the General persisted, and five minutes later we were all outside on the lawn and trucks were being sent for so that their headlights could provide illumination, and sixty-four of us were being thrust into our positions, and the General was shouting orders through cupped hands from the veranda.

'Taking the time from me! Right, pipers? It's p'fickly simple. S'easy. One, two, an' off we go!'

It was a nightmare, it really was. I had avoided being in the sixty-four; from where I was standing it looked like a crowd scene from *The Ten Commandments*, with the General playing Cecil B. de Mille. Officers, mess waiters, batmen, swung into the dance as the pipes shrilled, setting to partners, circling forwards and back, forming an enormous ring, and heughing like things demented. The General bounded about the veranda, shouting; the pipe-sergeant hurtled through the sets, pulling, directing, exhorting; those of us watching clapped and stamped as the mammoth dance surged on, filling the night with its sound and fury.

It took, I am told, one hour and thirteen minutes by the adjutant's watch, and by the time it was over the Fusiliers from the adjoining barracks were roused and lined along the wall, assorted Arabs had come to gaze on the wonders of civilization, and the military police mobile patrol was also on hand. But the General was tireless; I have a vague memory of him standing on the tailboard of a truck, addressing the assembled mob; I actually got close enough to hear him exhorting the pipe-sergeant in tones of enthusiasm and entreaty:

'Pipe-sarn't! Pipey! May I call you Pipey? ... never been done ... three figures ... think of it ... hunner'n-twenty-eightsome ... never another chance ... try it ... rope in the Fusiliers ... massed pipers ... regimental history ... please, Pipey, for me ...'

Some say that it actually happened, that a one hundred and twenty-eightsome reel was danced on the parade ground that night, General Sir Roderick MacCrimmon, KCB, DSO, and bar, presiding; that it was danced by Highlanders, Fusiliers, Arabs, military police, and three German prisoners of war; that it was danced to a conclusion, all figures. It may well have been; all I remember is a heaving, rushing crowd, like a mixture of Latin Carnival and Scarlett's uphill charge at Balaclava, surging ponderously to the sound of the pipes; but I distinctly recall one set in which the General, the pipe-sergeant, and what looked like a genuine Senussi in a burnous, swept by roaring, 'One, two, three,' and I know, too, that at one point I personally was part of a swinging human chain in which my immediate partners were the Fusiliers' cook-sergeant and an Italian café proprietor from down the road. My memory tells me that it rose to a tremendous crescendo just as the first light of dawn stole over Africa, and then all faded away, silently, in the tartan-strewn morning.

No one remembers the General leaving later in the day, although the Colonel said he believed he was there, and that the General cried with emotion. It may have been so, for the inspection report later congratulated the battalion, and highly commended the pipe-sergeant on the standard of the officers' dancing. Which was a mixed pleasure to the pipe-sergeant, since the night's proceedings had been an offence to his orthodox soul.

'Mind you,' he would say, 'General MacCrimmon had a fine agility at the pas-de-bas, and a decent sense of the time. Och, aye, he wass not bad, not bad ... for a Campbell.'

Night Run to Palestine

I HAD two grandmothers, one Presbyterian, the other pagan. Each told me stories, in her own way. The pagan, an incredibly old, bright-eyed creature from the Far West, peopled the world with kelpies and pixies and giants, or fair cold princesses and their sea-rover lovers; these were the tales her people had brought in the long ships centuries ago. And sometimes she would tell of our more immediate mainland ancestors, of the Red Fox and Robin Roy Macgregor and the caterans of the Highlands and the dirty tricks they played each other. But always her stories were full of passion and fighting and magic and cunning stratagems, and above all, laughter. Watching her old, wrinkled face, so eager, and the play of her ancient thin hands, it was easy to believe that her own grandmother had known a woman who had seen the men coming back from the '45 thrusting their broadswords into the thatch for another time, and stamping while the tears ran down their faces. Afterwards she would give me a penny or a potato scone, which she baked with great skill.

My other grandmother had only one story, the point of which eludes me still. She was a Glencoe MacDonald, strong and of few words, worshipping a stern God on whom she kept a close eye to see that He didn't get up to anything the Presbytery wouldn't have approved of, like granting salvation to Catholics and Wee Frees. She frightened me, for she was hard and forbidding and insisted that we walk miles to church on Sundays. On these walks I was naturally

forbidden to take my ball; on weekdays I could dribble it
along beside her, and on one occasion she even condes-
cended to kick it, watching it with a cold eye to see that it
rolled straight. It did. And it was on that occasion that she
told me the story; the sight of a distant train puffing along
the hillside had brought it to mind.

It appears that on the West Highland railway near Tyndrum there was a steep hill. A train of cattle in open trucks
was steaming up it, when a coupling broke and the
trucks began to run back down hill. In the rear truck was
the elderly guard and a young assistant, and the guard, as
the train gathered speed, cried to the young man :

'When you see me shump, you shump too. Better to be
killed on the bank than smochtered among the cattle.'

They had both jumped, and the young man broke his
ankle and the old guard smashed his watch, and the train
thundered on to the bottom of the hill and glided gradually
to a stop in perfect safety.

At this point my grandmother paused, and I waited for
the punchline. She stood gazing out across the glen with
that stony look that she would fasten on the minister if he
looked like letting up in his sermon after a mere forty minutes; her mind was away somewhere else.

'And that,' she said impressively at last, 'is what happened on the West Highland railway.'

I thought it was a pretty feeble story then, and it doesn't
look much better in retrospect, although I have a feeling
she saw a point to it which she didn't explain. But both
the story and that grim old lady who told it come back to
me every time I smell engine smoke or hear a whistle wail.
I have remembered it on the long haul across the prairies,
where the horizon stretches out for ever; on the sweaty
Punjab Mail, jam-packed inside with white-robed Orientals,
with more on the roof and in the windows and doorways
and fat babus clinging for dear life a yard above the tracks;
in the damp, blacked-out, blue-lit corridors of wartime
trains clanking on and halting interminably; in football

specials carrying the raucous, boozed-up supporters to Wembley; in a huge German train rattling across France with its solemn script notices, like ancient texts, telling you that pots were to be found under the seats, by order; in little trains at country halts, where beyond the misted windows you could see the glare of the porters' lamps and hear the sudden bang of a carriage door and the lonely call of 'Symington!' or 'Tebay!'

Most of all I remembered it on the Cairo–Jerusalem run in 1946 or '47, when the Stern Gang and the Irgun were at large, and the windows were sometimes boarded because the glass had been shot out, and lines were being blown up, and the illegal immigrant ships were coming in through the blockade, and a new nation was being uncomfortably born in a welter of hatred and confusion and total misunderstanding on all sides. Ben Hecht was having a holiday in his heart every time a British soldier died, and British soldiers were having a holiday in theirs at the prospect of getting away from a country they detested, in which some kind of illusion was shattered for them because the names of Bible stories had turned out to be places where machine-pistols rattled and grenades came in through windows. In the UN there was much talk and seeking of viable solutions and exploration of channels, and in the Palestine clubs young subalterns danced with their guns pushed round out of the way but still handy.

It was my gun that had got me into trouble. I had been on a course up at Acre – one of those courses where you walk miles across stony hills and look at maps, and a Guards officer instructor says, 'Now this is the picture ...' – and I was staying one night in Cairo before flying on to the battalion, which was living away along the North African coast, blancoing itself and playing football hundreds of miles from the shooting. Being me, I set off for the airport in the morning without my pistol, which was in the transit camp armoury, and so I missed my plane. You simply could not travel in those days without your gun; not that it was dangerous where I was going. It was just The Law. So I turned back for it, and the movements officer had a fit. Missing a plane was practically a capital charge. Apart from that, I couldn't get another for several days, so they looked for something unpleasant for me to do while I was waiting.

'You can be OC train to Jerusalem tonight,' said the Movements Officer, with sadistic satisfaction. 'Report to Victoria station at twenty-two hundred hours, don't be late, and this time take your blasted gun with you.'

So I had a bath, played snooker against myself all afternoon, and in the neon-lit Cairo evenfall rolled up to Victoria, clutching my little pistol in a damp palm. I fought my way through a press of enormous dragomans – huge, ugly people with brass badges who offer to carry your kit, and when you agree they whistle up some tiny assistant who shoulders your trunks and staggers off like an ant under a haystack. The dragoman doesn't carry anything; he just clears a way, roaring, and demands an exorbitant fee.

The movements office gave me a great sheaf of documents, a few instructions on how to command a troop train, reminded me that we left at ten sharp, and waved me away. The place looked like a stock market during a boom, everyone was running and shouting and chalking on boards; I got out to the bar, where sundry well-wishers cheered me up with anecdotes about the Jerusalem run.

'Tell me they're blowing one train in three,' said an American Air Corps major.

'Doing it dam' neatly, too,' said a captain in the Lincolns. ''Course, most of 'em are British or American-trained. On our side a year or two ago.'

A quartermaster from the South Lancs said the terrorists' equipment and stores were of the finest: Jerry landmines, piles o' flamin' gun-cotton, and more electrical gear than the GPO.

'Schmeiser machine-pistols,' said the American cheerfully. 'Telescopic sights. Draw a bead on your ear at six hundred yards with those crossed wires – then, bam! You've had it. Who's having another?'

'Trouble is, you can't tell friend from foe,' said the Lincoln. 'No uniforms, dam' nasty. Thanks, Tex, don't mind if I do. Well, thank God they don't get me past Gaza again; nice low demob group, my number'll be up in a month or two. Cheers.'

I said I had better be getting along to my train, and they looked at me reflectively, and I picked up my balmoral, dropped my papers, scrabbled them up, and went out in search of Troop Train 42, Jerusalem via Zagazig, Gaza and Tel Aviv, officer commanding Lt MacNeill, D., and the best of luck to him.

The platform was jammed all along its narrow length; my cargo looked like the United Nations. There were Arab Legion in their red-checked head-cloths, leaning on their rifles and saying nothing to anybody, ATS giggling in little groups and going into peals of laughter at the attempts of one of them to make an Egyptian tea-seller understand that she didn't take milk; service wives and families on the seats, the women wearing that glassy look of worn-out boredom and the children scattering about and bumping and shrieking; a platoon of long bronzed Australians, bush-hatted and talking through their noses; worried-looking majors and red-faced, phlegmatic corporals; at least one brigadier, red-tabbed, trying to look as though he was thinking of something important and was unaware of the children who were playing tig round him; unidentified semi-military civilians of the kind you get round bases – correspondents, civil servants, welfare and entertainment organizers; dragomans sweeping majestically ahead of their porters and barking strange Arabic words. Hurrying among them, swearing pathetically, was a fat little man with RTO on his sleeve and enormous khaki shorts on his withers; he seized on me and shouted above the noise of people and escaping steam.

'Stone me! You MacNeill? What a blasted mess! You've

got the short straw, you have. Fourteen Service families, Gawd knows how many kids, but they're all in the manifest. ATS an' all. I said we shouldn't have it, ought to be eighty-per-cent troops on any troop train, but you might as well talk to the wind that dried your first shirt.' He shoved another sheaf of papers at me. 'You can cope anyway. Just don't let any of 'em off before Jerusalem, that's all. There's at least two deserters under escort, but they're in the van, handcuffed. It's the civvies you've got to watch for; they don't like taking orders. If any of 'em get uppity, threaten to shoot 'em, or better still threaten to drop 'em off in a nice stretch of desert – there's plenty. Damn my skin, I'm misting up again!' He removed his spectacles from his pug nose, wiped them on a Service hankie, and replaced them; he was running sweat down his plump red cheeks. 'Now then, there's a padre who's worried about the ATS, God knows why, but he knows his own mind best, I dare say; keep an eye on the Aussies, but you know about them. And don't let the wog who's driving stop except at stations – that's important. If he tries, don't threaten to shoot *him*, just tell him he'll lose his pension. An' remember, you're the boss; to hell with ranks, they don't count on a train. You're the skipper, got it?'

The loudspeaker boomed overhead.

'Attention, please, attention. Will Captain Tanner please go to platform seven, plat-form sev-en. Captain Tanner, please.'

'All right, all right,' said the little man, savagely. 'I can only be one place at a time, can't I? Where was I? Oh, yes, you've a second-in-command, over there.' He pointed to a figure, standing alone near the engine. 'One of your crowd,' he added, looking at my tartan shoulder-flash. 'Seems all right. Sergeant Black!' he shouted, and the figure came over to us.

He was about middle height, with the big spreading chest and shoulders you often see in Highland regiments; his chin was blue and his profile was like a Red Indian's under the tilted bonnet with its red hackle. He was neat, professional, and as hard as a gangster, and he had the MM in front of the Africa and Italy ribbons. A pair of stony eyes looked me over, but he didn't say anything.

'The run takes seven hours,' went on the RTO. He stopped and shuffled his papers. He was thinking. 'If you hit trouble,' he said at last, 'you use your initiative. Sorry it's not much help, but there you are. You've got some signallers, and the telegraph line's never far away. You'll be OK as far as Gaza anyway; after that there's more chance of ... well, anyway, it's not likely there'll be any bother.'

The loudspeaker crackled again for Captain Tanner.

'Oh, shut up!' he snapped. 'Honest, it's the only blasted name they know. Well, look, you're off in about ten minutes. Better start getting 'em aboard. I'll get a bleat for you on the tannoy. Best of luck.' He hurried off, and then turned back. 'Oh, one other thing; there's a captain's wife with a baby and she thinks it's getting German measles. I wouldn't know.'

He bustled off into the crowd, and as he disappeared I felt suddenly lonely and nervous. One train, two hundred people — a good third of them women and children — seemed a lot of responsibility, especially going into a country on fire with civil strife and harried by armed terrorist gangs. Two deserters, a worried padre, and possible German measles. Oh, well, first things first. How does one start clearing a crowded platform into a train?

'Sergeant Black,' I said, 'have you made this trip before?'

'No, sir.'

'Oh. I see. Well, start getting them aboard, will you?'

God bless the British sergeant. He flicked his bonnet with his hand, swung round, and thundered, 'All aboard for Jerusalem,' as though he had been a stationmaster all his life. The tannoy boomed into sound overhead, and there was a general move towards the train. Sergeant Black moved in among the crowd, pointing and instructing — he seemed to know, by some God-given instinct, what to do — and I went to look at the engine.

I'm no authority, but it looked pretty rickety, and the genial Arab driver seemed to be in the grip of some powerful intoxicating drug. He had a huge laugh and a glassy eye, spoke no English, and fiddled with his controls in a reckless, unnerving way. I thought of asking him if he knew the way to Jerusalem, but it would have sounded silly, so I climbed into the front carriage, dumped my hand baggage on a seat in the compartment marked 'OC Train, Private' (with the added legend 'Kilroy was here — he hated it') and set off down the corridor to tour the train.

It was like the lower gun-deck of *The Fighting Téméraire* at Trafalgar, a great heaving mass of bodies trying to sort themselves out. There were no Pullman cars, and the congestion in the carriage doorways was brutal. I worked my way through to the guard's van, and found Sergeant Black eyeing the two deserters, tow-headed ruffians handcuffed to a staple on the wall.

'Let them loose,' he was saying to the MP escort.

'I'm responsible . . .' the MP began, and Black looked at him. There was one of those pregnant silences while I examined the instructions on the fire extinguisher, and then the MP muttered some defiance and unlocked the handcuffs. Sergeant Black lit a cigarette and tapped the butt of his Luger.

'See, you two,' he said. 'Run for it, and I'll blow yer — heids aff.' He caught sight of me and nodded. 'Awright this end, sir.'

'So I see,' I said and beckoned him out in the corridors. 'You think it's safe to loose those two?'

'Well, it's like this. If there's trouble, its no' right they should be tied up.'

'You mean if we hit the Stern Gang?'

'Aye.'

I thought about this, but not for long. There would certainly be other, more important decisions to make on the journey, and there was no point in worrying myself at this stage about the security of two deserters who were hardly likely to take off into the desert anyway. So I allotted Sergeant Black the rear half of the train, struggled back to my place at the front, checked my notorious pistol to see that it was loaded, satisfied myself that everyone was off the platform, and settled down with *The Launching of Roger Brook*, which was the current favourite with the discerning literati, although closely challenged by two other recent productions, *Animal Farm* and *Forever Amber*. The train suddenly heaved and clanked, and we were off.

The Cairo–Jerusalem run is one of the oldest and most well-worn routes in the world. By train in those days you went due north towards the Nile Delta and then swung east through Zagazig to Ismailia on the Canal. Then north along the Canal again to El Kantara, 'the Bridge' by which Mary and Joseph travelled and before them Abraham. Then you are running east again along the coast, with the great waste of the Sinai on your right and the Mediterranean on your left. This was the way the world walked in the beginnings of recorded time, Roman, Arab, Assyrian, Greek; if you could talk to everyone who used this road you could write the history of the human race. Everyone was here, except the Children of Israel who made it the hard way, farther south. And now they were trying to make it again, from a different direction, over the sea from Europe and elsewhere – still the hard way, they being Jews.

The track sticks to the coast as far as the Palestine border, where the names become familiar, echoing childhood memories of Sunday school and the Old Testament – Rafa and Gaza and Askalon away to the left, where the daughters of the uncircumcised were getting ready to cheer for Goliath; and then the line curves slowly away from the coast to Lydda, and doubles almost back on itself for the last lap south and east into Jerusalem.

At various points along the route Samson had destroyed the temple, Philip had begun preaching the gospel, Herod had been born, the Lord smote the thousand thousand Ethiopians, Peter cured in the name of Jesus, Solomon dreamed of being wise, and Uzziah broke down the walls of Jabneh. And Lt MacNeill, D., was following in their footsteps with Troop Train 42, which just shows that you can always go one better.

We had just rattled through Zagazig and Roger Brook was squaring up to the finest swordsman in France when there was a knock at my door and there stood a tall, thin man with a big Adam's apple knocking on his dog collar, wearing the purple-edged pips of the Royal Army Chaplain's Department. He peered at me through massive horn-rims and said:

'There are ATS travelling on this train.'

I admitted it; and he sucked in his breath.

'There are also officers of the Royal Air Force.'

His voice was husky, and you could see that, to his mind, Troop Train 42 was a potential White Slave Special. In his experience, RAF types and ATS were an explosive formula.

'I shouldn't worry, Padre,' I said, 'I'm sure . . .'

'But I must worry,' he said indignantly. 'After all, if we were not in this train, it would be time for Lights Out. These young girls would be asleep. The young men . . .' he paused; he wasn't so sure about the young men. 'I think that, as OC train, you should ensure that a curfew of compartments is observed after eleven o'clock,' he finished up.

'I doubt if there's any regulation . . .'

'You could enforce it. You have the authority.'

That was true enough: an OC train, however junior in rank, is like the captain of a ship; obviously he exercises tact where big brass is concerned, but when the chips are down he is the man. But authority cuts two ways. Now that I'd been reminded of it, I resented having a young sky-pilot (he was ribbonless and under thirty), telling me my job. I got formal.

'A curfew would be impractical,' I said. 'But I shall be patrolling the train from time to time, as will my sergeant.'

You could see he was wondering about that, too. He looked at me doubtfully and muttered something about spiritual duty and promiscuity. Plainly he was a nut. After shifting from one foot to the other for a moment, he bade me goodnight unhappily, and lurched off down the corridor, colliding with a fresh-faced young flight-lieutenant who was coming the other way. The RAF type was full of bonhomie, duty-free in the Service.

'Hiya, Padre,' said he. 'Playing at home this weather, eh?'

'I beg your pardon?'

'Well, this is your territory, isn't it?' said the youth. 'Y'know, bound for the Holy Land. Genesis, Exodus, Leviticus, Jezebel,' he waved expansively, 'Goliath of Gath, Sodom and Gomorrah and Gomorrah and Gomorrah creeps in this petty pace from day to day ...'

I went inside quickly and closed the door. Something told me the padre was going to have a worrying trip.

He wasn't the only one, although it was past El Kantara that the next interruption came. I had taken a trip along the train, and seen that everyone was reasonably installed for the night, conferred with Sergeant Black, and come back to my compartment. Roger Brook had pinked the villain long ago, and was now rifling the Marquis' closet for the secret plans, when the knock came.

It was a small ATS, blonde and snub-nosed, wearing two stripes. She saluted smartly and squeaked at me.

'Please, sir, could something be done about our carriage window? It's broken and boarded up, and Helen is in a draught. Actually, we all are, sir; it's very cold. But Helen feels it most.'

A young officer appealed to by ATS is a sorry sight. He becomes tremendously paternal and dignified, as only a twenty-one-year-old can. Elderly staff officers look like babbling lads beside him. He frowns thoughtfully, and his voice drops at least two octaves. I was no exception.

'Very good, corporal,' I said, sounding like Valentine Dyall with a heavy cold. 'Show me the way, please.'

She bounced off, with me following. Her billet was two coaches behind, and as we entered the second one I glanced into a compartment and found the padre staring at me with a mistrustful eye. *Quis custodiet*, by gum, he was thinking, so to assure him that all was well I gave him a big smile and the OK sign, thumb and forefinger together, other fingers raised. A second after I did it, I realized that it was open to misunderstanding, but it was too late then.

There were seven other ATS in the compartment, shivering, with the wind whistling through the boarded window. They emitted cries, and while the corporal told them it was OK now, because the OC train would fix it in person, I ploughed through their piles of kitbags, shoes, parcels, and general clutter to the window. There was a big crack in the boarding, but it looked as though it could be forced to quite easily.

'Can you manage, sir?' they cried. 'Will it shut?' 'I'm freezing.' 'Help him, Muriel.'

I heaved at the board and the whole damned thing came loose and vanished into the Palestine night. A tremendous blast of cold night air came in through the empty window. They shrieked.

'Oh, he's broken it!'

'Oh, it's perishing!'

'These Highlanders,' said a soulful-looking ATS with an insubordinate sniff, 'don't know their own strength.'

'Take it easy,' I said, nonplussed, to coin a phrase. 'Er, corporal, I think they'd better all move into the corridor ...'

'Into the corridor!' 'We can't stay there all night.' 'We're entitled to a compartment' – even in the ATS they had barrack-room lawyers, yet.

'. . . into the corridor until I get you fixed in other compartments,' I said. 'You can't stay here.'

'Too right we can't.' 'Huh, join the ATS and freeze to death.' 'Some people.' Mutters of mutiny and discontent while they gathered up their belongings.

I tramped out, told the corporal to keep them together, and, if possible to keep them quiet, and headed up the train. There was a compartment, I remembered, with only two officers in it. I knocked on its door, and a pouchy eye looked out at me.

'Well, what is it?' He was a half-colonel, balding and with a liverish look. I explained the situation.

'I thought you might not object if, say, four of the girls came in here, sir. It's one of the few compartments that isn't full.' Looking past him, I could see the other man, a major, stretched out on a seat.

'What? Bring ATS in here?'

'Yes, sir, four of them. I can get the other four placed elsewhere.'

'This is a first-class compartment,' he snapped. 'ATS other ranks travel third.'

'Yes, I know, but their compartment hasn't got a window . . .'

'Then I suggest you find them one that has.'

'I'm afraid there isn't one; they're all full.'

'That is your business. And I would point out that you have no right to suggest that they move in here.'

'Why not, for Pete's sake? Look,' I said, trying to sound reasonable, 'they have to go somewhere . . .'

'Don't address me in that way,' he barked. 'What's your name?'

'MacNeill.'

'Macneill what?'

He had me there. 'MacNeill, sir.'

He gave me a nasty look. 'Well, MacNeill, I suggest that you study the regulations governing the movement of troops trains. Also the limitations of authority of damned young whippersnappers who are put in charge of them, but are not, strange as it may seem, empowered to address their superiors in an insolent manner, or request them to vacate their compartments in favour of ATS.'

'I didn't ask you to vacate your compartment, sir,' I said, my voice shaking just a little, as it always does when I'm in that curious state halfway between backing down shame-faced and belting somebody. 'I merely asked, since they *are* women. . .'

'Don't dam' well argue,' said the man lying on the seat, speaking for the first time.

'No,' said the pouchy half-colonel. 'Don't argue, if you know what's good for you.' And he shut the door.

I stood there, hesitating. The choice was clear. I could fling open the door and give him a piece of my mind, taking the consequences, or I could creep off towards my own compartment. Eventually I compromised, creeping away and giving him a piece of my mind as I did so, in a reckless whisper. Not that it helped: the ATS were still homeless and had to be fitted in somewhere.

I needn't have worried. When I got back to the corridor where I had left them it was empty, but shrieks of female laughter led me to the primitive restaurant car, where they had found refuge with a mixed company of RAF and our gallant Australian cousins. From the way these two branches of the service were looking at one another it was obvious that the ATS were safer than they would have been in a convent; jealousy would see to that. Both sides were making heavy running, one big lean Aussie explaining to three of the ATS what a didgery-doo was, and offering them sips from his hip-flask, while my Biblical flight-lieutenant was leading the remainder in the singing of *Bless 'em all*, the revised version. I just hoped the padre was a sound sleeper.

Thereafter things were uneventful for about an hour. A fight broke out in one compartment because somebody snored; the soulful-looking ATS girl was sick – as a result, she insisted, of what the Australian had given her from his hip-flask; she hinted darkly that he had wanted to drug her, which seemed unlikely – a kitbag mysteriously fell from a window and the owner was only just prevented from pulling the communication cord, and one of the Arab Legion got locked in the lavatory. These things I observed on my hourly tour of the train; the Arab Legionnaire's predicament I came on after pushing through a small group of well-wishers singing 'Oh dear, what can the matter be?' I scattered them, and watched with interest while Sergeant Black painstakingly shouted orders through the locked door. It did no good; the entrapped one alternately bawled dreadful Arabic words and beat the panelling, and sent out a keening wail which was probably a lament that T. E. Lawrence hadn't minded his own business in the first place. Finally Black lost his temper and upbraided the man in purest Perthshire, at which the door flew open and the occupant, his face suffused, emerged with his rifle at the trail – why he had it with him he alone knew.

I congratulated Black and strolled back towards my compartment, speculating on whether there was an affinity between Arabic and the Crieff dialect, or whether the Arab had finally found how the bolt worked. I was pondering this in the corridor and listening to the rumbling ring of the wheels and looking through the window at the scrub-studded desert, black and silver in the moonshine, when the compartment door nearest me opened and a dishevelled young captain emerged, clutching a bundle. Beyond him a young woman was sitting with another bundle over her knees; both bundles were wailing plaintively and the compartment, which was otherwise unoccupied, was littered with clothes, towels, small clothes, utensils, and all the paraphernalia that an ignorant young bachelor associates with children.

'Yes, dear, I'll try,' the man was saying. 'There, there, Petey-Petey, all right, all right.'

'And it *must* be sterilized,' called the young woman, agitated. 'They must have some boiling water, somewhere. Yes, yes, Angie dear, mummy's going to fix it as soon as she possibly can ... Do hurry, dear, please!'

'Yes, darling, I *am* hurrying, as fast as I can. What shall I do with Petey?'

'Not on the seat!' cried the mother. 'He'll roll off!'

'Oh, God!' said the man, wild-eyed. He saw me. 'Have you any idea where there's boiling water?'

Some questions are best answered with a helpless gape.

'Please, Charles, hurry! Oh, no, Angela, did you have to?'

'She hasn't!' said the man, aghast.

'Oh, she has. Again. And I've only got a few clean ones left. Oh, Charles, do go for that water. It's past feeding-time. Oh, Angela.'

'Right dear. What shall I . . . ?' He wheeled on me. 'Look, can you hold Petey for a moment? I shan't be an instant.'

'Why, er . . .'

'Good man.' Harassed, he very gently passed the tiny bundle to me. It was stirring manfully, and letting out a noise that my toilet-locked Arab would have envied. 'Got him? Just like that: marvellous. I'm going, darling; this gentleman . . .'

'What? Oh, Angela, you little horror! Oh, really, I never knew babies could be so foul!'

'I'm leaving Petey with this . . . this officer,' cried the man. 'With Mr, er . . .'

'MacNeill.'

'Mr MacNeill. How d'ye do? My name's Garnett. This is my wife . . .'

'How do you do?' I said, clutching Petey tenderly.

'Charles! Please!'

'Yes, dear.' He grabbed a feeding-bottle and fled. Two seconds later he was back. 'Darling, where will I get the water?'

'Oh, darling, how do I know? The engine, or someplace. The train runs on boiling water, doesn't it?'

'Oh, yes,' he said, and fled again.

I sat down opposite Mrs Garnett. Angela, disrobed, was

lying across her knees squealing blue murder, while her mother, frantically sorting among the litter on the seat, cried endearments and shocking threats in turn. I turned Petey as though he were made of eggshells; I like babies, and the feel of his tiny, squirming body was somehow delightful. So was the tiny red face, all screwed up and raging as it was, eyes tight shut, minute toothless gums showing, and little legs kicking under his dress. My delight was temporary; I became aware that all was not well with Petey.

'Er,' I said. 'Er, I think Petey has . . .'

She seemed to see me for the first time. Normally she would have been a pretty, dark-haired young woman; now, clutching a nappy in one hand, and trying to steady her young with the other, her hair disordered and her manner disturbed, she looked like a gypsy wench preparing to attack a gamekeeper.

'Of course he has,' she snarled. 'They always do it together. I had to have twins! Oh, Angela, please lie still. Still, dearest! Mummy's trying to get you all comfy, you little monster! There, darling, Mummy has some nice, cool cream for iddums.' She was trying to tuck the nappy under Angela's midriff, and making rough work of it.

'But,' I said. 'What . . . I mean . . .' Petey was getting noxious. He suddenly changed gear in his screaming, taking up a new, intense note.

'Oh, dear, Petey-Petey!' She was distraught for her other young now. 'Just a minute, precious! Lie still, Angela, dearest, blast you! Well, don't just sit holding him! Do something!' She spared a hand to hurl nappies across. 'Change him, can't you?'

Ask me that question today, and rusty as I am with lack of practice, you will see an efficient response. I know the drill: newspaper on the floor, up with the dress, child face down and lightly gripped with the left hand; rubber pants down to knee-level with two swift pulls either side, pins out and thrust into the upholstery convenient to hand, nappy drawn down cleanly as child is slightly raised with left hand to permit front of nappy to come away; pause and gulp, drop nappy onto paper and fold paper over it with foot, mop the patient, anoint with cream to accompaniment of some rhythmic chant, whip clean nappy on and, with encouraging cries, pin one side, up and under, pin the other, make sure child has not been transfixed in process, up with rubber pants, and congratulations. Thirty seconds if you're lucky.

Today, yes, but this was many years ago, and all I knew of baby care was prodding them in the navel and saying 'Grrrtsh'. Changing nappies was outside my experience, and the way little Petey was delivering I wanted it to stay outside. Yet the British soldier is meant to be capable of anything. Could Wellington have changed a nappy? Or Marlborough? Doubtful. Or Slim? Yes, I decided, Slim could have changed a nappy, and almost certainly had. So for the honour of XIVth Army I began painfully and messily to strip Master Petey's abominable lower reaches, and in my innocence I sang him a lullaby at the same time – the old Gaelic one that goes *Hovan, hovan gorriago* and relates how the fairies stole away a baby from a careless mother. Mrs Garnett said that was all right with her, and what would they charge for twins?

So we worked away, myself the brutal soldier humming and coo-cooing, and the gentle mother opposite rebuking her daughter in terms that would have made a Marine corporal join the Free Kirk. And I was just pausing before the apparently impossible task of slipping a nappy on to the tiny creature, and marvelling at the very littleness of the squirming atom, with its perfect little fingers and their miniature nails, and pondering the wonder that he would probably grow into a great, hairy-chested ruffian full of sin and impudence, when the lights went out.

Mrs Garnett shrieked; I just clamped my hands as gently as I could on Petey and held on. My first thought, naturally enough, was of terrorists, until I realized that we were still a good way from the border, and the train was still rattling on. I assured her that everything was all right, and that Petey was in great shape – he wasn't, actually; he was at it again, spoiling all my good work – and presently the man Garnett came lumbering up the corridor, calling for directions and announcing that there was no hot water to be had, and what had happened to the lights.

It seemed to me I should be doing something about it, as OC train, so in the darkness I negotiated with him for the return of his infant, whom he accepted with exclamations of fatherly affection, changing to disgust, but by that time I was off roaring for Sergeant Black. I found him in the guard's van, with a candle and a fuse-box; he and an Arab in dungarees – who he was, heaven knows – were wrestling in the dark with wires, and presently the lights blinked back on again.

'Just a fuse,' he said. 'No panic.'

'Is that right?' I said. 'You try grappling with an independent baby in the dark. Which reminds me, there's a woman back there wants boiling water.'

'In the name of God,' said Sergeant Black. 'Is she havin' a wean?'

'Don't say that, even in jest,' I said. 'It's about all that hasn't happened on this bloody train so far. She wants to sterilize a feeding-bottle. How about it?'

He said he would see what he could do, pulled down his bonnet, and set off up the train. Within a quarter of an hour there was boiling water, feeding-bottles were being sterilized, and Mrs Garnett was being rapturously thankful. The sergeant had realized that although the restaurant car was without actual cooking appliances, there was at least a place where a fire could be lit.

After that there was peace until we reached the border. Black and I stood together at an open window near the front of the train, looking out over the desert and wondering about it. Up ahead was Gaza, where we were due for a stop; after that there was the Holy Land, where the Stern

Gang and the Irgun operated. I said that probably we wouldn't see any trouble; Black scratched his blue chin and said, 'Aye.' It was getting cold. I went back to my compartment and tried to get some sleep.

We drew into Gaza not long after, and everyone got off for tea or coffee at the platform canteen, except Black and the prisoners. We crowded the platform and I was half-way through my second cup and discussing child psychology with Captain Garnett when I suddenly realized that the crowd wasn't as thick as it had been five minutes before. But I didn't think they had got back on the train; where, then, were they going? Troops moving by train were confined to the platform at all halts; anywhere else was out of bounds. Oh, God, I thought, they're deserting.

They weren't, in fact. They were playing the Gaza Game, which was a feature of Middle East travel in those days. It worked like this. At Gaza, you changed your Egyptian pounds for the Military Administration Lire (mals) used in Palestine. The exchange rate was, say, 100 mals per £E1 at the currency control post on Gaza station. But if you knew the Game, you were aware that in a back street a few hundred yards from the station there dwelt Ahmed el Bakbook of the Thousand Fingers, otherwise Ahmed the Chatterer, who would give 120 mals per £E1. So you went to him, changed your £E to mals, hastened to the control office, changed your mals back to £E, raced off to Ahmed again, did another change, and so on until you had to board the train, showing a handsome profit. How the economies of Egypt and Palestine stood it I wouldn't know, nor yet how Ahmed made a living at it. But that was how it worked, as I discovered when I was investigating the sudden exodus from the platform, and was accosted by the pouchy lieutenant-colonel who claimed to have detected several soldiers sneaking out of the station. Oh, he knew what they were up to, all right, he said, and what was I doing, as OC train, to stop it? I was keen enough on finding ATS girls billets to which they were not entitled, but I appeared to be unable to control the troops under my command. Well, well, and so on.

Personally, I couldn't have cared less if the troops had changed the entire monetary reserves of Egypt into roubles, at any rate of exchange, but technically he was right, which was why I found myself a few moments later pounding down a dirty back alley in Gaza, damning the day I joined the Army. In a dirty shop, easily identified by the khaki figures furtively sneaking in and out, I confronted a revolting Arab. He was sitting at a big plain table, piled with notes and silver, with an oil lamp swinging overhead and a thug in a burnous at his elbow.

He gave me a huge smile, all yellow fangs and beard, and said, 'How much, lieutenant?'

'You,' I said, 'are conducting an illegal traffic in currency.'

'Granted,' he replied. 'What do you require?'

'Dammit,' I said. 'Stop it.'

He looked hurt. 'Is not possible,' he said. 'I fill a need. That is all.'

'You'll be filling a cell in Acre jail when the military police get wise to you,' I said.

'Everyone gets out of Acre jail, you know?' he said cheerfully. 'And you do not suggest I work in defiance of the military police? They do not trouble me.'

He was just full of confidence, a little amused, a little surprised. I wondered if I was hearing right.

'Come on, old boy, get a move on,' said a voice behind. One of the RAF types was standing there with his wallet out. 'Time presses, and all that. And you did jump the queue, you know.'

I gave up. Ahmed dealt courteously with the RAF type, and then asked me almost apologetically how much I wanted to change. I answered him coldly, and he shrugged and dealt with the next customer. Then he asked me again, remarked that it must be getting near train time, and since I had already infringed the regulations myself by leaving the station, I might as well take advantage of his unrivalled service.

He was right, of course, this good old man. I shovelled across my £E, accepted his mals, declined his invitation to join him in a draught of Macropoulos' Fine Old Highland Dew Scotch Whisky – 'a wee deoch-and-dorus', as he called it – and fled back to the station. I had no time to make another transaction, but I looked in at the currency office to see how trade was going, and asked the Royal Army Pay Corps sergeant if he was not worried about getting six months on the Hill at Heliopolis for knowingly assisting the traffic in black market exchange.

'Don't make me laugh,' he said. 'I'm buyin' a pub on the Great West Road when I get my ticket.'

My lieutenant-colonel was still on the platform. He had watched several score military personnel leave the station, he said, and I had done nothing that he could see to stop them. Would I explain? His manner was offensive.

I asked him what he, as an officer, had done about it himself, he went pale and told me not to be impertinent, and after a few more exchanges I said rudely that I was not responsible to him for how I conducted the affairs of Troop Train 42, and he assured me that he would see that disciplinary action was taken against me. I got on the train again shaking slightly with anger and, I admit it, apprehension, and ran slap into the padre, who was all upset about the ATS still.

I needed him. Perhaps I was overwrought, but I told him rather brusquely to stop bringing me unnecessary complaints, to mind his own business, to go back to his compartment, and generally to get off my neck. He was indignant, and shocked, he said. I advised him again to go back to his compartment, and he said stiffly that he supposed he must take my orders, but he would certainly make a report ...

'All right, Padre,' I said. 'Do that. But for the present

just remember that to obey is better than sacrifice, and hearkening than the fat of rams. OK?'

He said something about the Devil and Scripture, and I went back to my compartment pretty depressed. It seemed suddenly that I had loused things up fairly substantially: two rockets were on the way, I had failed to control the troops efficiently at Gaza, I hadn't covered myself with glory in accommodating the ATS, I couldn't even change a nappy. What was I good for? I lay down and fell asleep.

Your real hero can sleep through an elephant stampede, but wakes at the sound of a cat's footfall. I can sleep through both. But the shriek of ancient brakes as a train grinds violently to a halt wakes me. I came upright off the seat like a bleary panther, groping for my gun, knowing that something was wrong and trying to think straight in a second. We shouldn't be stopping before Jerusalem; one glance through the window showed only a low, scrubby embankment in moon-shadow. As the wheels screamed to a halt I dived into the corridor, ears cocked for the first shot. We were still on the rails, but my mind was painting vivid pictures of a blocked line and an embankment stiff with sharp-shooters.

I went through the door to the platform behind the tender; in the cabin I could see the driver, peering ahead over the side of his cab.

'What the hell is it?' I shouted.

He shouted back in Arabic, and pointed ahead.

Someone was running from the back of the train. As I dropped from the platform to the ground he passed through the shaft of light between two coaches and I recognized Black's balmoral. He had his Luger out.

He slowed down beside me, and we went cautiously up past the engine, with the little wisps of steam curling up round us. The driver had his spotlight on, and the long shaft lit up the line, a tunnel of light between the embankment walls. But there was nothing to see; the embankment itself was dead still. I was turning to ask the driver what

was up when he gave an excited little yelp behind us. Far
down the track, on the edge of the spotlight beam, a red
light winked and died. Then it winked again, and died.

A hoarse voice said, 'Get two men with rifles to the top
of the bank, either side. Keep everyone else on the train.
Then come back here.'

It had almost finished speaking before I realized it was
my own voice. Black faded away, and a moment or two
later was back.

'They're posted,' he said.

I wiped my sweaty hand on my shirt and took a fresh
grip of the revolver which I ought to have remembered
back in Cairo, so that some other mug could have been
here, playing cops and robbers with Bert Stern or whoever
it was. 'Let's go,' I said, just like Alan Ladd if he was a
soprano. My hoarse voice had deserted me.

We walked up the line, our feet thumping on the sleepers,
the spotlight behind us throwing our shadows far ahead,
huge grotesques on the sand. The line 'The dust of the
desert is sodden red' came into my head, but I hadn't time
even to think the uncomfortable thought about it when
he just materialized in front of us on the track, so suddenly
that I was within an ace of letting fly at him. I know I
gasped aloud in surprise; Black dropped on one knee, his
Luger up.

'Hold it!' It was my hoarse voice again, sounding loud
and nasty. And with the fatal gift of cliché that one invariably displays in such moments, I added, 'Don't move or
I'll drill you!'

He was a young man, in blue dungarees, hatchet-faced,
Jewish rather than Arab. His hands were up; they were
empty.

'Pliz,' he said. 'Friend. Pliz, friend.'

'Cover him,' I said to Black, which was dam' silly, since
he wasn't liable to be doing anything else. Keeping out of
line, I went closer to him.

'Who are you?'

'Pliz,' he said again. He was one of these good-looking, black-curled Jews; his mouth hung open a bit. 'Pliz, line brok'.' And he pointed ahead up the track.

I left Black with him, collected the driver and his mate, and went off up the track. Sure enough, after a little search we found a fish-plate unscrewed and an iron stake driven between the rail ends – enough to put us off the track for sure. I didn't quite realize what that signified until the driver broke into a spate of Arabic, gesturing round him. I looked, and saw we were out of the cutting; now the ground fell away from the track on both sides, a rock-strewn slide that we would have crashed down.

While the driver and his mate banged out the stake and got to work on the fish-plate, I went back to where Black had the young Jew in the lee of the engine. There was a small crowd round them, contrary to my orders, but one of them – an Arab Legion officer – was talking to him in Hebrew, and getting results.

'What's he say?' I asked.

'Oh, God, he's a dope,' said the officer. 'He found the rail broken, I think, and heard the train coming. So he stopped us.'

'He found the rail broken? In the middle of the bloody night? What was he doing here?'

'He doesn't seem to know.' He directed a stream of Hebrew at the youth and got one back, rather slower. The voice was thick, soft.

'Don't believe a word of it,' a voice was beginning, but I said, 'Shut up,' and asked the officer to translate.

'He was looking for a goat. He lives in a village some-where round here.' It sounded vaguely Biblical; what was the story again . . . the parable of the shepherd . . .

'What about the red light?' It was Sergeant Black.

Questioned, the youth pulled from his pocket a lighter and a piece of red cellophane.

'For God's sake,' I said.

'He's probably a bloody terrorist,' said someone.

'Don't be a fool,' I said. 'Would he warn us if he was?'

'How dare you call me a fool?' I realized it was my old friend the pouchy half-colonel. 'Who the—'

'Button your lip,' I said, and I thought he would burst. 'Who authorized you to leave the train? Sergeant Black, I thought I gave you orders?'

'You did, sir.' Just that.

'Then get these people back on the train – now.'

'Now, look here, you.' The half-colonel was mottling. 'I'll attend to you in due course, I promise you. Sergeant, I'm the senior officer: take this man' – he indicated the Jew – 'and confine him in the guard's van. It's my opinion he's a terrorist . . .'

'Oh, for Heaven's sake,' I said.

'. . . and we'll find out when we get to Jerusalem. And you,' he said to me, 'will answer for your infernal impudence.'

It would have been a great exit line, if Sergeant Black had done anything except just stand there. He just waited a moment, staring at the ground, and then looked at me.

'OC train, sir?' he said.

I didn't catch on for a moment. Then I said, 'Carry on, sergeant. Take him aboard. Get the others aboard, too – except those who want to stand around all night shooting off their mouths in a soldier-like manner.' What had I got to lose?

I went up the track, to where the driver was gabbling away and yanking fiercely on a huge spanner. He gave me a great grin and a torrent of Arabic, from which I gathered he was coming on fine.

I went back to the train: Sergeant Black was whistling in the sentries from the banks; everyone was aboard. Presently the driver and his mate appeared, chattering triumphantly, and as I climbed aboard the engine crunched into life and we lumbered up track. The whole incident had occupied about ten minutes.

In the guard's van Black and the Arab Legion captain and

my half-colonel were round the prisoner – that's what he was, no question. The captain interrogated him some more, and the half-colonel announced there was no doubt about it, the damned Yid was a terrorist. To the captain's observation that he was an odd terrorist, warning trains instead of wrecking them, he paid no heed.

'I hold you responsible, sergeant,' he told Black. 'He must be handed over to the military police in Jerusalem for questioning, and, I imagine, subsequent trial and sentence. You will ...'

'You won't hold my sergeant responsible,' I said. 'I'll do that. I'm still in command of this train.'

For a moment I thought he was going to hit me, but unfortunately he didn't. He just bottled his apoplexy and marched out, and the captain went with him, leaving me and Black and the Jew. The two deserters, I supposed, were farther up the train. We were rattling along at full clip now; Black reckoned we were maybe two hours out of Jerusalem. I gave him a cigarette, and nodded over to the window.

'Well?' I said. 'What d'you make of him?'

He took off his bonnet and shook his cropped head.

'He's no terrorist, for certain,' I said. 'Well, ask yourself, is he?'

'I wouldnae know. He looks the part.'

'Oh, come off it, sergeant. He warned us.'

'Aye.' He dragged on the cigarette. 'What was he doin' there, in the middle of the night?'

'Looking for a goat.'

'In dungarees stinkin' o' petrol. Aye, well. And makin' signals wi' a lighter an' cellophane. Yon's a right commando trick for a farmer. That yin's been a sodger, you bet. Probably wi' us, in Syria, in the war.'

'But he doesn't speak English.'

'He lets on he disnae.' He smiled. 'And if you're lookin' for goats, ye don't go crawling aboot on yer belly keekin' at fish-plates, do ye?'

'You think he knew, before, about the broken rail?'

'I'm damned sure of it, sir. Yon was a nice, professional job. He knew aboot it, but why he tellt us . . . search me.'

I looked over at the Jew. He was sitting with his head in his hands.

'He told us, anyway,' I said. 'Whether he's a terrorist or not, or knows terrorists, doesn't much matter.'

'It'll matter tae the military police in Jerusalem. Maybe they've got tabs on him.'

'But, dammit, if he is a Stern Gangster, why the hell would he stop the train?'

Black ground out his cigarette and looked me in the face. 'Maybe he's just soft-hearted. Maybe he doesnae want tae kill folk after all.'

'Who are you kidding? You believe that?'

'Look, sir, how the hell dae I know? Maybe he's a bloody boy scout daein' his good deed. Maybe he's no' a' there.'

'Yes,' I said. 'Maybe.' It was difficult to see any rational explanation. 'Anyway, all we have to do is see that he gets to Jerusalem. Then he's off our backs.'

'That's right.'

I hesitated about telling Black to keep a close eye on him, and decided it was superfluous. Then I went back up the train, full of care, noticing vaguely that the two deserters were in a group playing rummy, and that the blinds were down on the padre's compartment. Captain and Mrs Garnett had their door open, and were talking animatedly; in the background one of the twins was whimpering quietly.

'But, darling.' he was saying. 'German measles isn't serious. In fact, it's a good thing if they get it when they're little.'

'Who says?'

'Oh, medical people. It's serious if you get it when you're older, if you're a girl and you're pregnant. I read that in *Reader's Digest*.'

'Well, who's to say it's true? Anyway, I'm worried about

Angie now, not ... not twenty years hence. She may never get married, anyway, poor little beetle.'

'But it may not be German measles, anyway, darling. It may be a nappy rash or something ...'

Everybody had their troubles, including the formerly incarcerated Arab legionnaire, who was now trying to get *into* the lavatory, and wrestling with the door handle. The young pilot officer was lending a hand, and saying, 'Tell you what, Abdul, let's try saying "Open Sesame" ...'

All was well with the ATS, the Australians, and the airmen; the excitement caused by our halt had quieted down, and I closed my compartment door hoping nothing more would happen before we got to Jerusalem. How much trouble could the pouchy half-colonel make, I wondered. The hell with him, I had been within my rights. Was the young Jew a terrorist, and if he was, why had he stopped the train? And so on, and I must have been dozing, for I remember being just conscious of the fact that the rhythm of the wheels had changed, and we were slowing, apparently to take a slight incline, and I was turning over on the seat, when the shot sounded.

It was a light-calibre pistol, by the sharp, high crack. As I erupted into the corridor it came again, and then again, from the back of the train. An ATS shrieked, and there were oaths and exclamations, and I burst into the guard's van to find Sergeant Black at the window, his Luger in his hand, and the smell of burned cordite in the air. The train was picking up speed again at the top of the incline. The Jew was gone.

'What the hell ...' I was beginning, and stopped. 'Are you all right?'

He was standing oddly still, looking out at the desert going by. Then he holstered his gun, and turned towards me.

'Aye, I'm fine. I'm afraid he got away.'

'The Jew? What happened?'

'He jumped for it. When we slowed down to take the hill. Went out o' that windae like a hot rivet, and doon the bank. I took a crack at him, two or three shots ...'

'Did you hit him?'

'Not a chance.' He said it definitely. 'It's no use shootin' in this light.'

There were people surging at my back, and I wheeled round on them.

'Get back to your carriages, all of you! There's nothing to get alarmed about.'

'But the shooting . . .' 'What the hell . . .'

'There's nothing to it,' I said. 'A prisoner jumped the train, and the sergeant took a pot at him. He got away. Now, go back to your compartments and forget it. We'll be in Jerusalem shortly.'

Through the confusion came Old Inevitable himself, the pouchy half-colonel, demanding to know what had happened. I told him, while the others faded down the corridor, and he wheeled to the drawling major, who was at his elbow, and bawled:

'Stop the train!'

'Now, take it easy,' I said. 'There's no point in stopping; he's over the hills and far away by now, and he's a lot less important than the safety of this train. We're not stopping until we get to Jerusalem.'

'I'll decide that!' he snapped, and he had an ugly, triumphant look as he said it. 'You've lost the prisoner, in spite of my instructions, and this train is being stopped . . .'

'Not while I command it.'

'You don't! You're a complete bloody flop! I'm taking over. John, pull that communication . . .'

It must have been pure chance, but when the Major turned uncertainly to touch the communication cord, Sergeant Black was right in his way. There was one of those pregnant silences, and I jumped into it.

'Now look, sir,' I said to the half-colonel. 'You're forgetting a few things. One, I *am* OC train, and anyone who tries to alter that answers to a general court-martial. Two, I intend to report you to the GOC for your wilful hampering of my conduct of this train, and your deliberate disobedience of orders from properly constituted authority.'

'Damn you!' he shouted, going purple.

'You left the train when we halted, in flat defiance of my instructions. Three, sir, I've had about my bellyful of you, sir, and if you do not, at once, return to your compartment, I'm going to put you under close arrest. Sir.'

He stood glaring and heaving. 'Right,' he said, at last. He was probably wondering whether he should try, physically, to take over. He decided against it. 'Right,' he said again, and he had his voice under control. 'Major Dawlish, you have overheard what has been said here? Sergeant, you are a witness . . .'

'Aye, sir,' said Black. 'I am that.'

'What do you mean?' snapped the half-colonel, catching Black's tone. 'Let me tell you, Sergeant, you're in a pretty mess yourself. A prisoner in your . . .'

'Not a prisoner,' I said. 'A man who had warned us about the railway line and was being carried on to Jerusalem, possibly for interrogation.'

He looked from me to Black and back again. 'I don't know what all this is about,' he said, 'but there's something dam' fishy here. You,' he said to me viciously, 'are going to get broken for this, and you, Sergeant, are going to have a great deal of explaining to do.' He wheeled on his buddy. 'Come along, John.' And they stumped off down the corridor.

When they had gone I lit a cigarette. I was shaking. I gave another one to Black, and he lit up, too, and I sat down on a box and rested my head on my hand.

'Look,' I said. 'I don't understand it either. But there is something dam' fishy, isn't there? How the hell did he get away?'

'I told ye, sir. He jumped.'

'Oh, yes, I know. But look, sergeant, let's not fool around. Between ourselves, I'm not Wild Bill Bloody Hickock, but he couldn't have broken from me, so I'm damned sure he couldn't break from you. People as experienced as you, I mean, you carry a Luger, you know?'

He said, poker-faced, 'I must have dozed off.'

I just looked at him. 'You're a liar,' I said. 'You never dozed off in your life – except when you wanted to.'

His head came up at that, and he sat with smoke trickling up from his tight mouth into his nostrils. But he didn't say anything.

'What are we going to tell them in Jerusalem?' I said.

'Just what I told you, sir. He was a gey fast mover.'

'You could get busted,' I said. 'Me, too. Oh, it'll be well down my crime-sheet, after tonight. I've done everything already. But it could be sticky down at your end too.'

He smiled. 'My number's up in the next couple of months. I've got a clean sheet. I'm no' worried about being busted.'

He seemed quite confident of that. He looked so damned composed, and satisfied somehow, that I wondered if perhaps the exigencies of the journey had unhinged me a little.

'Sergeant Black,' I said. 'Look here. The man was a terrorist – you think so, anyway. Well, why on earth ...'

'Yes, sir?'

'Never mind,' I said wearily. 'The hell with it.'

I knew what he was going to come back to. Terrorist or not, he had saved the train, and everyone on it, me and the pouchy half-colonel and Angie and Petey and the ATS and lavatory-locked legionnaires. Why, God alone knew. Maybe he hadn't meant to, or something. But I knew Black and I were speculating the same way, and giving him the benefit of the doubt, and thinking of what would have happened if he *had* been a terrorist, and there had been tabs on him in Jerusalem.

'The hell with it,' I said again. 'Sergeant, I'm out of fags. You got one?'

It was while I was lighting up and looking out at the desert with the ghostly shimmer that is the Mediterranean dawn beginning to touch its dark edges, that for no reason at all I remembered Granny's story about the cattle-train at Tyndrum. I suppose it was the association of ideas: people jumping from trains. I told Sergeant Black about it, and we discussed grannies and railways and related subjects, while the train rattled on towards Jerusalem.

Just before we began to run into the suburbs, the white buildings perched on the dun hillsides, Sergeant Black changed the topic of conversation.

'I wouldn't worry too much about yon half-colonel,' he said.

'I'm not worried,' I said. 'You couldn't call it worry. I've just got mental paralysis about him.'

'He might think twice about pushing charges against you,' said Black. 'Mind you, he stepped over the mark himsel'. He wouldnae come well out of a court-martial. And ye were quite patient wi' him, all things considered.' He grinned. 'Your granny wouldnae have been as patient.'

'Huh. Wonder what my granny would have said if she had been wheeled before the brigadier?'

'Your granny would have *been* the brigadier,' he said. 'We're here, sir.'

Jerusalem station was an even bigger chaos than Cairo had been; there were redcaps everywhere, and armed Palestine Police, and tannoys blaring, and people milling about the platforms. Troop Train 42 disgorged its occupants: I didn't see the half-colonel go, but I saw the Arab Legion forming up to be inspected, and Captain Garnett and his wife, laden with heaps of small clothes and handbags from which bottles and rolls of cotton wool protruded, carrying Angie and Petey in a double basket; and the ATS giggling and walking arm-in-arm with the Aussies and the RAF types, and the padre with loads of kit, bargaining with a cross-eyed thug wearing a porter's badge. Sergeant Black strode through the train, seeing everyone was off; then he snapped me a salute and said:

'Permission to fall out, sir?'

'Carry on, Sergeant,' I said.

He stamped his feet and hoisted his kitbag on to his shoulder. I watched him disappear into the crowd, the red hackle on his bonnet bobbing above the sea of heads.

I went to the RTO's office, and sank into a chair.

'Thank God that's over,' I said. 'Where do I go from here? And I hope it's bed.'

The RTO was a grizzled citizen with troubles. 'You Mac-Neill?' he said. 'Troop Train 42?'

'That's me,' I said, and thought, here it comes. Pouchy had probably done his stuff already, and I would be requested to report to the nearest transit camp and wait under open arrest until they were ready to nail me for — let's see — insubordination, permitting a prisoner to escape, countenancing illegal trafficking in currency, threatening a superior, conduct unbecoming an officer in that I had upbraided a clergyman, and no doubt a few other assorted offences that I had overlooked. One way and another I seemed to have worked my way through a good deal of the prohibitions of the Army Act: about the only one I could think of that I hadn't committed was 'unnatural conduct of a cruel kind, in that he threw a cat against a wall'. Not that that was much consolation.

'MacNeill,' muttered the RTO, heaving his papers about. 'Yerss, here it is. Got your train documents?' I gave them to him. 'Right,' he said. 'Get hold of this lot.' And he shoved another pile at me. 'Troop Train 51, leaves oh-eight-thirty for Cairo. You'll just have time to get some breakfast.'

'You're kidding,' I said.

'Don't you believe it, boy,' he said. 'Corporal Clark! Put these on the wire, will you? And see if there's any word on 44, from Damascus. Dear God,' he rubbed his face. 'Well, what are you waiting for?'

'You can't put me on another train,' I said. 'I mean, they'll be wanting me for court-martial or something.' And I gave him a very brief break-down.

'For God's sake,' he said. 'You were cheeky to a half-colonel! Well, you insubordinate thing, you. It'll have to keep, that's all. You weren't the only one who was getting uppish last night, you know. Some people gunned up a convoy near Nazareth, and apart from killing half a dozen of us they did for a United Nations bigwig as well. So there's activity today, d'you see? Among other things, there aren't enough perishing subalterns to put in charge of troop trains. Now, get the hell out of here, and get on that train!'

I got, and made my way to the buffet, slightly elated at the idea of making good my escape on the 8.30. Not that it would do any good in the long run; the Army always catches up, and the half-colonel was the vindictive sort who would have me hung if it took him six months. In the meantime I wasn't going to see much of the famous old city of Jerusalem; eating my scrambled eggs I wondered idly if some Roman centurion had once arrived here after a long trek by camel train, only to be told that he was taking the next caravan out because everyone was all steamed up and busy over the arrest of a preaching carpenter who had been causing trouble. It seemed very likely. If you ever get on the fringe of great events, which have a place in history, you can be sure history will soon lose it as far as you are concerned.

I got the 8.30, and there was hardly a civilian on it; just troops who behaved themselves admirably except at Gaza, where there was the usual race in the direction of Ahmed's back-street banking and trust corporation; I just pretended it wasn't happening; you can't fight international liquidity. And then it was Cairo again, just sixteen hours since I had left it, and I dropped my papers with the RTO, touched my revolver butt for the hundred and seventeenth time to make sure I still had it, and went back to the transit camp, tired and dirty. I went to sleep wondering where the escaping Jew had got to by this time, and why Sergeant Black had let him go. It occurred to me that the Jew might have had a pretty rough time in Jerusalem, what with everyone's nerves even more on edge with the Nazareth business. Anyway, I wasn't sorry he had got away; all's well that ends well; I slept like a log.

All hadn't ended well, of course; two mornings later a court of inquiry was convened in an empty barrack-room at the transit camp, to examine the backsliding and evil behaviour of Lieutenant MacNeill, D., and report thereon. It consisted of a ravaged-looking wing-commander as president, an artillery major, a clerk, about a dozen witnesses, and me, walking between with the gyves (metaphorically) upon my wrists. The redcap at the door tried to keep me out because I didn't have some pass or other, but on finding that I was the star attraction he ushered me to a lonely chair out front, and everyone glared at me.

They strip a man's soul bare, those courts of inquiry. With deft, merciless questioning they had found out in the first half-hour not only who I was, but my rank and number; an officer from the transit camp deponed that I had been resident there for several days; yet another certified that I had been due out on such-and-such a flight; an airport official confirmed that this was true, and then they played their master card. The pilot of the aircraft (this is sober truth) produced an affidavit from his co-pilot (who was unable to attend because of prickly heat) that I had not, to anyone's knowledge, boarded the plane, and that my seat had been given to Captain Abraham Phillipowski of the Polish Engineers, attached to No 117 Field Battery, Ismailia.

They were briefly sidetracked because the president plainly didn't believe there was such a person as Captain Abraham Phillipowski, but once this had been established to their satisfaction the mills of military justice ground on, and another officer from the transit camp described graphically my return after missing the plane, and my dispatch to Jerusalem.

The president wanted to know why I had been sent to Jerusalem; witness replied that they had wanted to keep me employed pending a court of inquiry into why I had missed the plane; the president said, pending this court, you mean;

witness said yes, and the president said it seemed bloody silly to him sending a man to Jerusalem in between. Witness said huffily it was no concern of his, the president said not to panic, old boy, he had only been making a comment, and witness said all very well, but he didn't want it appearing in the record that he had been responsible for sending people to Jerusalem when he hadn't.

The president suggested to the clerk that any such exchange be deleted from the record (which was assuming the proportions of the Greater London telephone directory, the way the clerk was performing with his shorthand), and I unfortunately coughed at that moment, which was taken as a protest. A judicial huddle ensued, and the president emerged, casting doubtful glances at me, to ask if I had anything to say.

'I forgot my gun,' I said.

He seemed disappointed. 'He forgot his gun,' he repeated to the clerk.

'I heard,' said the clerk.

'All right, all right!' cried the president. 'Keep your hair on.' He looked at me. 'Anything else?'

'Should there be?' I asked. It seemed to me that they hadn't really started yet, but I wasn't volunteering information about events on the train, which seemed to me to dwarf such trivia as my missing my plane in the first place.

'Dunno,' said the president. He turned to the clerk. 'How do we stand, old boy?'

'He forgot his gun, he missed the plane,' said the clerk bitterly. 'That's what we're here to establish. What more do you want?'

'Search me,' said the president. 'You did miss the plane, didn't you?' he asked me.

'That's irregular,' bawled the clerk. 'At least, I think it is. You're asking him to convict himself.'

'Rot,' said the president. 'He hasn't been charged, has he? Anyway, old boy, you're mixing it up with wives not being able to testify against their husbands.'

'I need a drink,' said the clerk.

'Good show,' said the president. 'Let's adjourn, and then you can type all this muck out and we'll all sign it. Any objections, objection overruled. Smashing.'

The proceedings of that court occupied about forty-five minutes, and heaven knows how many sheets of foolscap, but it did establish what it had set out to do – that I had negligently failed to take a seat on an aircraft. It was all carefully forwarded to my unit, marked attention Commanding Officer, and he blew his stack, mildly, and gave me three days' orderly officer for irresponsible idiocy – not so much for missing the aircraft as for causing him to waste time reading the report. But of Black, and the escaping Jew, and threats, and insubordination, and currency offences there was never a word.

And, as my grandmother would have said, that is what happened on the Cairo–Jerusalem railway.

The Whisky and the Music

THE ignorant or unwary, if asked whether they would rather be the guests of an officers' mess or a sergeants', would probably choose the officers'. They might be motivated by snobbery, but probably also by the notion that the standards of cuisine, comfort, and general atmosphere would be higher. They would be dead wrong.

You will get a bit of the old *haut monde* from the officers in most units, although in a Highland regiment the native savagery has a tendency to show through. I remember the occasion when two Guards officers, guests of our mess, were having a delicate Sunday morning breakfast and discussing Mayfair and the Season with the adjutant, himself an exquisite, when there entered the motor transport officer, one Elliot, a hard man from the Borders. Elliot surveyed the table and then roared:

'Naethin' but toast again, bigod! You,' he shouted at the adjutant, 'ye bloody auld vulture, you, ye've been gobblin' my plain bread!' And he wrenched the adjutant's shirtfront out of his kilt, slapped him resoundingly on the solar plexus, and ruffled his hair. This was Elliot's way of saying good morning, but it upset the Guards. They just looked at each other silently, like two Jack Bennys, and then got slowly to their feet and went out, looking rather pale.

That would never happen in a sergeants' mess. Sergeants are too responsible. They tend to be young-middle-aged soldiers, with a sense of form and dignity; among officers there is always the clash of youth and age, but with sergeants you have a disciplined, united front. And whereas the provisioning and amenities of an officers' mess are usually in the hands of a president who has had the job forced on him and isn't much good at it, your sergeants look after their creature comforts with an expertise born of long service in hard times. Wherever you are, whoever goes short, it won't be the sergeants; they've been at the game too long.

Hogmanay apart, officers never saw inside our sergeants' mess ('living like pigs as we do,' said the Colonel, 'it would make us jealous'), so when Sergeant Cuddy of the signals section invited me in for a drink I accepted like a shot. We had been out in the desert on an exercise, and Cuddy and I had spent long hours on top of a sand-hill with a wireless set, watching the company toiling over the sun-baked plain below, popping off blanks at each other. Cuddy was a very quiet old soldier with silver hair; his first experience of signals had been with flags and pigeons on the Western Front in the old war, and I managed to get him to talk about it a little. It emerged that he had heard of, although he had not known, my great-uncle, who had been a sergeant with the battalion at the turn of the century.

'There'll be a picture of him in the mess,' said Cuddy. And then, after a long pause, he added: 'Perhaps ye'd care to come in and see it, when we go back to barracks?'

'Will it be all right?' I asked, for regimental protocol is sometimes a tricky thing.

'My guest,' said Cuddy, so I thanked him, and when we had packed up the exercise that afternoon I accompanied him up the broad steps of the whitewashed building just outside the barracks where the sergeants dwelt in fortified seclusion.

In the anteroom there was only the pipe-sergeant, perched in state at one end of the bar, and keeping a bright eye on the mess waiters to see that they kept their thumbs out of the glasses.

'Guest. Mr MacNeill,' announced Cuddy, and the pipey hopped off his stool and took over.

'Come away ben, Mr MacNeill,' he cried. 'Isn't this the pleasure? You'll take a little of the creature? Of course, of course. Barman, where are you? Stand to your kit.'

I surveyed the various brands of 'the creature' on view behind the bar, and decided that the Colonel was right. You would never have seen the like in an officers' mess. There was the Talisker and Laphroaig and Islay Mist and Glenfiddich and Smith's Ten-year-old – every Scotch whisky under the sun. How they managed it, in those arid post-war years, I didn't like to think.

I'm not a whisky man, but asking for a beer would have been unthinkable; I eventually selected an Antiquary, and the pipe-sergeant raised his brows and pursed his lips approvingly.

'An Edinburgh whisky,' he observed judicially. 'Very light, very smooth. I'm a Grouse man, myself.' He watched jealously as the barman poured out the very pale Antiquary and gave me my water in a separate glass (if you want to be a really snob whisky drinker, that is the way you take it, in alternate sips, a right 'professional Highlander' trick). Then we drank, the three of us, and the pipe-sergeant discoursed on whisky in general – the single malts and the blends, and 'the Irish heresies', and strange American concoctions of which he affected to have heard, called 'Burboon'.

Sergeant Cuddy eventually interrupted to say that I had come to view the group photographs lining the mess walls, to see my great-uncle, and the pipe-sergeant exclaimed in admiration.

'And he was in the regiment? God save us, isn't that the thing?' He bounded from his stool and skipped over to the row of pictures, some of them new and grainy-grey, others deepening into yellow obscurity. 'About when would that be, sir? The Nineties? In India? Well, well, let's see. There's the '02, but that was in Malta, whatever they were doing there. Let's see – Ross, Chalmers, Robertson, McGregor – all the teuchters, and look at the state of them, with their bellies hanging over their sporrans. I'd like to put *them* through a foursome, wouldn't I just.' He went along the row, Cuddy and I following, calling out names and bestowing comments.

'South Africa, and all in khaki aprons. My, Cuddy, observe the whiskers. Hamilton, Fraser, Yellowlees, O'Toole – and what was he doing there, d'ye suppose? A right fugitive from the Devil's Own, see the bog-Irish face of him. Murray, Johnstone –'

'I mind Johnstone, in my time,' said Cuddy. 'Killed at Passchendaele.'

'— Scott, Allison – that'll be Gutsy Allison's father, Cuddy. Ye mind Gutsy.' The pipe-sergeant was searching out new treasures. 'Save us, see there.' He pointed to a picture of the Twenties. 'Behold the splendour there, Mr Macneill.' I looked at a face in the back rank, vaguely familiar, grim and tight-lipped. 'He's filled out since then,' said the pipe-sergeant. 'Seventeen stone of him now, if there's an ounce. That's our present Regimental Sergeant-Major. Anderson, McColl, Brand, Hutcheson—'

'Hutcheson got the jail,' said Cuddy. 'He played the fiddle for his recreation, and went poaching with snares made from violin strings. An awfy man.'

They chattered on, or at least the pipey chattered, and I made polite murmurs, and at last they ran my great-uncle to earth, reclining at the end of a front row and showing his noble profile in the Victorian manner. Showing as much of it, anyway, as was visible through his mountainous beard: he gave the impression of one peering through a quickset hedge.

'Fine, fine whiskers they had,' cried the pipe-sergeant admiringly. 'You don't get that today. Devil the razor there must have been among them, the wee nappy-wallahs of India must have done a poor, poor trade at the shaving, I'm thinking. He's a fine figure, your respected great-uncle, Mr MacNeill, a fine figure. Ye have the same look, the same keek under the brows, has he not, Cuddy? See there,' and he pointed to the minute portion of ancestor that showed through the hair, 'isn't that the very spit? Did ye know him, sir?'

'No,' I said. 'I didn't. He died in South Africa, of fever, I think.'

'Tut, tut,' said the pipe-sergeant. 'Isn't that just damnable? No proper medical provisions then, eh, Cuddy?'

I was studying the picture — 'Peshawar, 1897', it was labelled — and thinking how complete a stranger one's closest relative can be, when a voice at my elbow said formally:

'Good evening, sir,' and I turned to find the impressive figure of the RSM beside me. He nodded in his patriarchal style — even without his bonnet and pace-stick he was still a tremendous presence — and even deigned to examine great-uncle's likeness.

'If he had lived I would have known him,' he said. 'I knew many of the others, during my boy service. You have a glass there, Mr MacNeill? Capital. Your good health.'

The mess was beginning to fill up now, and as we chatted under the pictures one or two others joined us — old Blind Sixty, my company quartermaster, and young Sergeant McGaw, who had been organizer of a Clydeside Communist Party in civilian life. 'How's Joe Stalin these days?' demanded the pipe-sergeant, and McGaw's sallow face twitched into a grin and he winked at me as he said, 'No' ready tae enrol you, onyway, ye capitalist lackey.'

They gagged with each other, and presently I finished my drink and straightened my sporran and said I should be getting along . . .

'Have you shown Mr MacNeill his forebear's other portrait?' demanded the RSM, and the pipey, at a loss for once, said he didn't know there was one. At which the RSM moved majestically over to the other wall, and tapped a fading print with a finger like a banana. 'Same date, you see,' he said, ''97. This is the battalion band. Now, then . . . there, Pipe-Sergeant MacNeill.' And there, sure enough, was the ancestor, with his pipes under his arm, covered in hair and dignity.

The pipe-sergeant squeaked with delight. 'Isn't that the glory! He wass a pipe-sergeant, *the* pipe-sergeant, like myself! And hasn't he the presence for it? You can see he is just bursting with the good music! My, Mr MacNeill, what pride for you, to have a great-uncle that wass a pipe-sergeant. You have no music yourself, though? Ach, well. You'll have a suggestion more of the Antiquary before ye go? Ye will. And yourself, Major? Cuddy? McGaw?'

While they were stoking them up, the RSM drew my attention to the band picture again, to another figure in the ranks behind my great-uncle. It was of a slim, dark young piper with a black moustache but no beard. Then he traced down to the names underneath and stopped at one. 'That's him,' he said. 'Just a few months, I would say, before his name went round the world.' And I read, 'Piper Findlater, G.'

'Is that *the* Findlater?' I asked.

'The very same,' said the RSM.

I knew the name from childhood, of course, and I suppose there was a time when, as the RSM said, it went round the world. There was the little jingle that went to our regimental march, which the children used to sing at play :

> *Piper Findlater, Piper Findlater,*
> *Piped 'The Cock o' the North',*
> *He piped it so loud*
> *That he gathered a crowd*
> *And he won the Victoria Cross.*

There are, as Sapper pointed out, 'good VCs' and ordinary VCs – so far as winning the VC can ever be called ordinary. Among the 'good VCs' were people like little Jack Cornwell, who stayed with his gun at Jutland, and Lance-Corporal Michael O'Leary, who took on crowds of Germans single-handed. But I imagine if it were possible to take a poll of the most famous VCs over the past century Piper George Findlater would be challenging for the top spot. I don't say that because he was from a Highland regiment, but simply because what he did on an Afghan hillside one afternoon caught the public imagination, as it deserved to, more than such things commonly do.

'Well,' I said. 'My great-uncle was in distinguished company.'

'Who's that?' said the piper, returning with the glasses. 'Oh, Findlater, is it? A fair piper, they tell me – quite apart from being heroical, you understand. I mind him fine – not during his service, of course, but in retirement.'

'I kent him weel,' said Old Sixty. 'He was a guid piper, for a' I could tell.'

'A modest man,' said the RSM.

'He had a' the guts he needed, at that,' said McGaw.

'I remember the picture of him, in a book at home,' I said. 'You know, at Dargai, when he won the VC. And then it came out in a series that was given away with a comic-paper.'

'Aye,' said the pipe-sergeant, on a triumphant note, and everyone looked at him. 'Everybody kens the story, right enough. But ye don't ken it all, no indeed, let me tell you. There wass more of importance to Findlater's winning the cross than just the superfeecial facts. Oh, aye.'

'He's at it again,' said Old Sixty. 'If you were as good at your trade as ye are at bletherin', ye'd have been King's Piper lang syne.'

'I'd be most interested to hear any unrelated facts about Piper Findlater, Pipe-sergeant,' said the RSM, fixing him with his eye. 'I thought I was fully conversant wi' the story.'

'Oh, yes, yes,' said the pipey. 'But there is a matter closely concerned with regimental tradition which I had from Findlater himself, and it's not generally known. Oh, aye. I could tell ye.' And he wagged his head wisely.

'C'mon then,' said McGaw. 'Let's hear your lies.'

'It's no lie, let me tell you, you poor ignorant Russian lapdog,' said the pipey. 'Just you stick to your balalaikeys, and leave music to them that understands it.' He perched himself on the arm of a chair, glass in hand, and held forth.

'You know how the Ghurkas wass pushed back by the Afghans from the Dargai Heights? And how our regiment wass sent in and came under torrents of fire from the wogs, who were snug as foxes in their positions on the crest? Well, and then the pipers wass out in front – as usual – and Findlater was shot through first one ankle and then through the other, and fell among the rocks in front of the Afghan positions. And he pulled himself up, and crawled to his pipes, and him pourin' bleed, and got himself up on a rock wi' the shots pourin' away round him, and played the regimental march so that the boys took heart and carried the crest.'

'Right enough,' said Old Sixty. 'How they didn't shoot him full of holes, God alone knows. He was only twenty yards from the Afghan sangars, and in full view. But he never minded; he said after that he was wild at the thought of his regiment being stopped by a bunch o' niggers.'

Sergeant McGaw stirred uncomfortably. 'I don't like that. He shouldn't have called them niggers.'

'Neither he should, and you're right for once,' said the pipey. He sipped neatly at his glass. 'They wass not niggers; they wass wogs. Any roads, they carried him oot, and Queen Victoria pinned the VC on him and said: "You're a canny loon, Geordie", and he said, "You're a canny queen, wifie", and—'

The RSM snorted. 'He did nothing of the sort, Pipe-sergeant.'

'Well, not in so many words, maybe,' conceded the pipey. 'But here's what none of you knows. The papers wass full of it, how he had played the regimental march under witherin' fire, and *Cock o' the North* was being sounded up the length and breadth of the land, in music-halls, and by brass bands, and by street fiddlers, and every-

body. The kids wass singing it. And Findlater, when his legs
wass mended, suddenly took thought, and said to his pal
the corporal piper, "Ye know, I'm no' certain, but I doubt it
wass the regimental march I played at all. I think it was
Haughs o'Cromdale."

'The corporal piper considered this, and cast his mind
back to the battle, and said Findlater was right. It wasnae
Cock o' the North at all, but he didnae think it was *Haughs
o' Cromdale* either; by his recollection it was *The Black
Bear*.

'They argued awa', and got naewhere. So they called on
the Company Sergeant-Major, who confessed he couldnae
tell one from t'ither, but thought it might have been *Bonnie
Dundee*.

'Finally, it got to the Colonel's ears, and he wass dis-
mayed. Here wass the fame of Piper Findlater ringing
through the land, and everyone talking about how he had
played *Cock o' the North* in the face of the enemy, and the
man himself wasnae sure what he had played at all. There
wass consternation throughout the battalion. "A fine thing
this," says the Colonel. "If this gets out we'll be the
laughing-stock o' the Army. Determine at once what tune
he played, and let's have no more damned nonsense."

'But they couldn't do it. Every man who had been within
earshot on the Dargai slope, as soon as you asked him, had
a different notion of what the tune was, but how could
they be sure, with the bullets flying and them grappling
with their bayonets against the Khyber knives? You have
to have a very appreciative ear for music to pay much heed
to it at a time like that. One thing they decided: there was
general agreement that whatever he played, it wasn't
Lovat's Lament.'

Lovat's Lament is a dirge; played with feeling it can make
Handel's Largo sound like the Beatles.

The pipe-sergeant beamed at us. 'Well, there it was. No
one was certain at all. So the Colonel did the only thing
there was to do. He sent for the Regimental Sergeant-Major.

'"Major," says he, "what did Piper Findlater play on the Dargai Heights?"

'The RSM never blinked. "*Cock o' the North*, sir," says he. "Ye're sure?" says the Colonel. "Positive," says the RSM. "Thank God for that," says the Colonel. And it was only later that it occurred to him that the RSM had not been within half a mile of Findlater during the battle, and couldn't know at all. But *Cock o' the North* the RSM had said, and *Cock o' the North* it has been ever since, and always will be.'

Sergeant McGaw made impatient noises. 'What the hell did it matter, anyway? They took the heights, and he won his VC. It would have been just the same if he had been playin' *Roll out the barrel*.'

The pipe-sergeant swelled up at once. 'You know nothing, McGaw. You have neither soul nor experience. Isn't it important that regimental history should be right, and that people shouldn't have their confidence disturbed? Suppose it was to transpire at this point that Nelson at Trafalgar had said nothing about England expecting, but had remarked instead that he was about due for leave, and once the battle was over it was him for a crafty forty-eight-hour pass?'

'Not the same thing at a',' said McGaw.

'You're descending to the trivial,' said the RSM.

'The country would degenerate at once!' cried the pipe-sergeant, and at this point I finally made my excuses, thanked them for their hospitality, and left them in the throes of philosophic debate.

Back in our own mess, I mentioned to the Colonel that I had been entertained by the sergeants, and had heard of the Findlater controversy. He smiled and said:

'Oh, yes, that one. It comes up now and then, not so often now, because of course the survivors are thinning out.' He sighed. 'He was a great old fellow, you know, Findlater. I used to see him going about. Indeed, touching on the pipe-sergeant's story, I even asked him once what he did play at Dargai.'

'What did he say?'

'Wasn't quite sure. Of course, he was an old man then. He had an idea it might have been *The Barren Rocks of Aden*. Or possibly *The 79th's Farewell to Gibraltar*. I had my own theory at one time, I forget why, that it must have been *The Burning Sands of Egypt*.'

I digested this. 'So it's never been settled, then?'

'Settled? Of course it has. He played *Cock o' the North*. Everyone knows that.'

'Yes, sir, but how do they know?'

The Colonel looked at me as at a rather dim-witted child. 'The RSM said so.'

'Of course,' I said. 'Foolish of me. I was forgetting.'

Guard at the Castle

IT is one of the little ironies of Army life that mounting guard is usually more of an ordeal than actually standing guard. And frequently the amount of anguish involved in mounting is in inverse proportion to the importance of the object to be guarded. For example, as a young soldier I have been turned out in the middle of the night in jungle country, unwashed, half-dressed, with a bully-beef sandwich in one hand and a rifle in the other, to provide an impromptu bodyguard for the great Slim himself; this was accomplished at ten seconds' notice, without ceremonial. On the other hand, I have spent hours perfecting my brass and blanco to stand sentry on a bank in Rangoon which had no roof, no windows, and had been gutted by the Japanese anyway.

This merely proves that Satan finds mischief for idle hands, and there are fewer hands idler than those of military authority outside the firing line.

Edinburgh Castle, from the guards' point of view, is in a class by itself. It is tremendously important, in a traditional rather than a strategic sense; if someone broke into it and pinched Mons Meg the actual well-being of the country would not be affected, but the blow to national prestige would be tremendous. The papers would be full of it. Consequently, providing a guard for the Castle involves – or used to – more frantic preparation, ceremonial, organization, and general nervous tension than the filming of *Ben Hur*. It is rather like a combination of putting on a Paris fashion display and planning a commando raid, and the fact that its object is to provide a skeleton guard which couldn't stop a marauding party of intelligent Brownies is, in the military view, beside the point.

It was a few months after our battalion had come home from the Middle East to be stationed near Edinburgh. It was one of those summers just after the war when there was gaiety and eagerness in the air, and the dark years were just behind and everyone was enjoying themselves. Princes Street was all sunshine and uniforms and pretty dresses, the American Fleet was in the Forth, royalty was coming to town, God was in His Heaven, and I was once again the battalion orderly officer. It was a restful job, wandering round barracks drinking cups of tea in the cookhouse, chivvying the Jocks out of the canteen at closing time, casting a critical eye at the guards and picquets, and generally taking life easy – until some genius in the High Command woke up one morning with the brilliant idea that during the royal visit, with distinguished American naval dignitaries also being on hand, it would be nice to have a Highland regiment on guard at the Castle. That meant us, and us meant me.

The turmoil that broke out from our orderly room was indescribable. The Colonel, that kindly, vulture-faced man who had looked Japanese guards in the face on the Moulmein Railway and said, 'No,' now became visibly agitated for the first time in living memory; he took me aside, addressed me as 'Young Dand,' twisted his moustache, and spoke rapidly and incoherently about the importance of putting on a good show. The adjutant got on the other side of me and rattled instructions into my ear, impressing the necessity of perfect organization, split-second timing, immaculate appearance, and perfect coordination. He gave me to understand that the slightest slip would mean the ruin of the regimental reputation and my own personal destruction, and exhorted me to keep calm.

Like every young officer in dire need, I went straight to

the Regimental Sergeant-Major, who drew up his enormous bulk an inch higher at the thought of exhibiting his perfections before royalty, soothed my hysterics, and suggested that we go through the drill. As he reminded me, it was perfectly simple; we had done it together scores of times without a hitch. All we needed was an intelligent guard consisting of a sergeant, corporal, and five good men, and we could take our pick of my company.

We went through the drill. What happens at guard-mounting is this: the orderly officer and RSM wait at one end of the parade ground, just in front of the object to be guarded – in our case the Castle gateway. The guard march on at the other end of the parade ground, and the RSM brings them to a halt roughly in its middle. He then invites the orderly officer to inspect them, and the pair of them march the fifty or so yards to the guard, look them over, and march back again. The RSM roars out more orders, the guard present their rifles for inspection, officer and RSM march forward again, look at the rifles, march back, and the RSM marches the guard into the Castle, the orderly officer standing off to one side and taking the salute. There is a pause of a couple of minutes, in which the officer has the parade ground to himself, then the old guard is marched out, briefly inspected, and marched off. The officer retires, and that is that. Easy; in our case the only difference was that a vast crowd, including royalty and a fearsome array of home and foreign brass, would be watching.

We summoned the Company Sergeant-Major, a hard-bitten Aberdonian, and he produced the list of men who were due for guard.

'You've got McAuslan down here,' I said.

'He's due,' said the CSM.

'He's overdue,' I said. 'I'd sooner go on guard with Laurel and Hardy.'

McAuslan, as I have explained, was one of those soldiers. He was short, pimply, revoltingly dirty, incredibly unseemly, and dense to a degree. Not that he didn't try; he was pathetically eager to please, but it was no good. His stupidity and uncleanliness were a sort of gift, and combined with his handlessness made him a military disaster. He had been twice forcibly washed by his comrades, and had never been off defaulters until it was discovered that punishment was wasted on him. The thought of having him on the Castle guard, out there in the sunlight, with royalty watching ...

'No,' I said. 'Lose him. Forget him. Get anyone you like, get one of the cooks, but not McAuslan.'

The CSM said he would see to it, and for two days my platoon barrack-room went at it as never before. The sergeant, corporal and five men were scrubbed, polished, drilled, examined, pleaded with, threatened, cajoled, and watched over like newborn chicks. I took them through the drill until they could have done it in their sleep; the best belts, tartans, cap badges, pouches, and small packs were borrowed from the ends of the battalion and worked on by the whole platoon; their boots were boned and polished till they gleamed like black diamonds; their rifles and bayonets were oiled and polished till they glittered; even their puttees were ironed, and when they stood up on the morning of the great day in the barrack-room, in all their glory, they were a lovely sight to see.

The RSM, the CSM and I buzzed round them, peering and pulling and encouraging them; the Colonel looked in, hummed, approved, got in the way, and was tactfully rebuked by the RSM; he fidgeted for a while, clicking his lighter and chewing his cigarette, and then said, 'All right, young Dand; good luck, lads, must be off,' and shot out — poor soul, he was going to be next to royalty, suffering agonies.

Then we waited. A truck was to take us to the Castle in about half an hour; I still had to get dressed, but my kit was all in order, with my batman standing guard on it, and for the moment we had the barracks almost to ourselves. The rest of the battalion were out on an exercise which was going on at Redford, and we sat in the silence, smoking and watching the sweat on the backs of our hands.

There was a clatter of boots in the corridor, the door opened, and I looked up to see McAuslan in the doorway. Amazingly he was dressed as for guard-mounting – that is, all his equipment was there, but in its usual state of rank disorder. You wouldn't have let him guard a coal-bunker.

'In Goad's name!' said the CSM. 'Whit are you on?'

'Guard, sir,' said McAuslan. His bonnet was squint, and there was an oil-stain on his shirt. He had perhaps washed his face three days ago.

'Guard?' echoed the RSM. 'Not you, my lad. You were taken off the rota days ago. Don't you look at the notice-board?'

'Ah cannae read,' said McAuslan.

'Aye, weel, ye can hear,' said the CSM. 'And ye're not on guard, nor likely tae be. Ye know why? Ye're dirty, ye're idle, an' – an' ye're a positive disgrace. Now, oot o' this and report to the quartermaster for fatigues.'

McAuslan, pimply and unkempt, wiped his nose and looked unhappy. For a minute I couldn't think why; not one man in that guard but would have gladly slipped out of it if he could; they were sitting quaking, and here was this tartan Caliban looking miserable at news that would have delighted any of them.

'All right, McAuslan,' I said. 'Carry on to the quarter-master.' And for some reason I found myself adding: 'Sorry.'

He went, and the truck rumbled up outside. I was just stubbing out my cigarette and preparing to go to my quarters to dress when it happened. I still see it in night-mares.

One of the guards, a stocky, dapper Glaswegian named Grant, had stretched himself and strolled to the door. What he put his foot on I don't know, but one moment he was standing, and then he was falling, and some evil spirit had caused a drum of yellow paint, used for marking kitbags, to be in a corner by the door, and one moment there was a beautiful soldier and the next there was a swearing creature whose kilt and left arm and left leg were a different colour. His comrades leaped back squealing like debs at Ascot.

We gazed at him appalled. Plainly he was beyond repair, there was no one else to take his place, we could not go on a man short – or so it seemed to me then, with military procedure drilled into my mind. I still had to dress, fool that I was to have left it so late, we had about five minutes – and royalty and the rest of them would be waiting. This was desperate. Where to find another man?

The RSM was looking at me. I looked from him to the CSM. We all had the same thought.

'My God!' I said.

'We cannae take him,' said the CSM.

'We must,' said the RSM, and lifted up his voice. 'Mc-Auslan!'

Two minutes later I was in my quarters, wrenching on my dress uniform, tearing at the kilt buckles, my batman blaspheming as he adjusted my sporran and buckled on my Sam Brown. Then I was running, the truck was at the door, I had a horrid vision of a pallid ragamuffin sitting opposite the RSM in the back being told the intricacies of guard drill – guard drill, to McAuslan, the man who thought slope arms was something to do with the Nazi salute.

I don't remember the drive through Edinburgh, mercifully; and to this day even my memories of Edinburgh Castle itself are hazy. I remember being there in the sunlight, before the gateway, and the murmur of a brightly coloured holiday crowd, and the little group of green-tartaned figures coming on at the other end, with McAuslan shachling in the middle of the rear rank, managing to swing his left arm in time with his left leg. (Try that, sometime; only McAuslan can do it.)

Then they halted, rigid in the heat haze, and the thunder of the RSM's voice broke the silence, and behind me I heard the mutter of the CSM – 'Goad, look at 'im. No two pun' of him hingin' straight.' I knew who he meant.

Then the RSM, huge and magnificent, was saluting in front of me, and my own voice was barking (surprisingly strong) and I came awake again, and paced across the vast distance to the guard.

They were doing well. They were all red in the face, and when you got near you could see them trembling, but they were standing up straight; they were with it. As I moved slowly along the front row I heard my own voice again, softly this time.

'Easy does it, now, easy. You're doing fine. Nothing to worry about. You're looking good, McFarlane, you're looking very good. Head up a wee bit, Nichol, that's it. You're a good-looking guard.' And behind me the RSM whispering: 'Next order is port arms. Take it steady.'

Now the second rank, and I was opposite McAuslan. The RSM and CSM had done their best, but I was thankful the spectators were a hundred yards away. His face was grimy, his boots were dull, his shirt and kilt appeared to have been slept in. When I got behind him I noticed his bayonet: there was a ring of rust between blade and sheath.

'Easy, McAuslan,' I said, and, God forgive me; 'You're looking fine.'

We marched back, the RSM and I, gave them port arms, and marched forward again. I made a pretence of looking at the rifles, which were held up for inspection, but no more than a glance, until we came to the second row. As I passed McAuslan – his rifle looked as though it had been at the bottom of the Monkland Canal for a month – I heard the RSM make a noise. If you think there is no such thing as a yelp and whisper combined, there is.

I looked, and nearly passed out. At port arms the rifle bolt is drawn back, exposing the magazine, and McAuslan's magazine had gleaming brass rounds in it. How he had managed this I still don't know, but there he was, with a loaded rifle, mounting guard at Edinburgh Castle. For a vivid moment the thought that he was going to assassinate royalty crossed my mind; then I realized, with mounting horror, that the guard's next manoeuvre was to 'ease springs', which involves working the bolt and finally pressing the trigger, which in McAuslan's case would mean scattering ·303 cartridges all over the place and probably blowing someone's head off.

But nothing is too much for an RSM. Deftly he reached over, detached McAuslan's magazine, and conjured it out of sight. Then we were marching back to our places, and I was just breathing again when I was aware of a curious sensation at my right hip.

You know how it is – not a pain, or even a touch, but just a feeling, as though something has been taken away. I felt, rather than heard, a slight snap, and instinctively clapped my right fist to my hip. There was a movement that was not the motion of marching; and for a few seconds I knew real, paralysing terror. One of my kilt buckles, wrenched in the hurry of dressing, had given way. There was a second one, of course, but was it fastened properly? I knew, with horrifying certainty, that if I removed my fist that vast, silent crowd would be treated to the edifying sight of a Highland officer marching in his shirt-tail while his kilt collapsed in ruins about his ankles. In that moment I really wanted to die.

I halted, turned, and shouted my orders, and then paced off to the side to take the salute. I was marching with right arm akimbo, and the military in the crowd must be wondering and whispering. I halted and turned, bringing my fist into my kidneys and clutching with my thumb; the guard came marching past, throwing on the style in their relief (McAuslan was swinging left arm and left leg together in fine abandon); their heads snapped round in salute – which I didn't return – and they had vanished into the gateway.

I was alone, with the worst to come. I had to turn again,

march to the edge of the crowd in front of the General Officer – with royalty beside him – salute, and march off again.
But I couldn't salute! My saluting hand was holding up my
nether garments, and if I removed it I should go down in
history as the Man Whose Kilt Fell off in Front of Royalty
At Edinburgh Castle.

It wouldn't do. Similarly, I could not march off without
acknowledging royalty and saluting. What do you do in
this case? I shall tell you. You turn smartly about, arm
akimbo – it gives a Rupert of Hentzau touch, anyway –
march up to the saluting base, salute left-handed, turn
about, and march off through the Castle gateway, dead
casual, like Caesar at Pharsalia.

In the guardroom was pandemonium. McAuslan, unseen
by me, had dropped his rifle in the gateway, the RSM had
caught it, McAuslan had turned round and asked for it
back, the RSM had almost thrown him into the guardroom,
and the corporal, a sensitive soul, had done a brief faint.

I waved them away. I had to go out again and take the
salute of the old guard going off; I had troubles.

'Give me that kilt, McFarlane,' I said.

He goggled at me.

'Come on, man, get it off.' I had my own off by now.

'But, sir, I'm first on stag . . .'

'Well, if the Russians come you can wave your shirt-tail
at them,' I snarled, more or less dragging the garment off
him. I was just buckling it on when the Colonel strode in,
full of joy and gladness. Royalty had thought we looked
nice; the General was pleased; the American admirals had
thought it was colossal; he was pleased; were we pleased?
We just looked at him.

'By the way, young Dand,' he added. 'Why were you
standing like a blasted ballet dancer at the finish?'

I told him. He went green, and then white, and then he
sat down on a bench to make little moaning sounds.

Meanwhile the CSM was addressing McAuslan. 'You get
your kit, and when the truck comes you get on it, and go

back to barracks, and stay there, oot o' sight, and if ye move wan step ...' Then he turned to me. 'I'll get him replaced, sir. We cannae have him standing sentry, look at the condeetion of him.'

I looked, and he was in a state. Apart from his natural foulness, he was in an extremity of terror, and looking thoroughly miserable. I was about to say: 'Carry on,' when suddenly it seemed all wrong and unfair.

'No,' I said. 'Not a dam' chance. He's mounted guard, he'll do guard. Right, McAuslan? Carry on, Sergeant-Major.'

I saw the old guard – Fusiliers, I think they were – off, and after that everything seemed peaceful, and none of it had ever happened. I think I slept most of the afternoon, and it wasn't until late evening that I went into the guard-room, and saw everything was in order, and it was just on sunset when I took a turn outside, and it was one of those evenings, with the black, gaunt battlements against the sky, and the lights of Edinburgh winking in the dusk below, and I found myself thinking of the generations of soldiers who had guarded this place, and the Gay Gordon, and Bonnie Dundee, and the rest of it.

I came to the gate, and there was the inheritor of the great tradition: they had given him a clean shirt, and someone had polished his boots, and he was looking less like an ill-tied sack than usual, but his face was still its customary grey, and he was standing sentry like a yokel with a pitch-fork.

He sloped arms as I came up, and in giving a butt salute managed to half drop his rifle. I helped straighten him out, and then turned away to breathe in the evening air. And then he spoke.

' 'Sa'right, i'nt it?' he said.

'What's that?'

' 'Sa'right. Guardin' ra Castle.'

I digested this. 'Yes,' I said. 'It's all right.'

He sighed heavily. 'Ah like it fine.'

'You know what to do?' I asked him.

'Oh, aye, sir. Wan-I-take-up-a-position-at-the-main-gate. Two-I-patrol—'

'Yes, yes, I know all that. That's by the book. But you know what to do if anyone tries to get past you?'

'Sure, sir. Ah'll kill the—'

'Well, yes. And turn out the guard.'

'Och, aye, sir.'

I left him standing there, and he was loving every minute of it, scruffy creature that he was. At the same time, I had nearly made a bigger fiasco of it than he, with all his natural talent, could ever have done.

At that moment I wouldn't have swapped McAuslan for the whole Household Cavalry.

McAuslan's Court-martial

CONSIDERING his illiteracy, his foul appearance, his habit of losing his possessions, and his inability to execute all but the simplest orders, Private McAuslan was remarkably seldom in trouble. Of course, corporals and sergeants had long since discovered that there was not much point in putting him on charges; punishment cured nothing, and, as my platoon sergeant said, 'He's just wan o' nature's blunders; he cannae help bein' horrible. It's a gift.'

So when I found his name on the company orders sheet one morning shortly after his Edinburgh Castle epic, I was interested, and when I saw that the offence he was charged with was under Section 9, Para 1, Manual of Military Law, I was intrigued. For that section deals with 'disobeying, in such manner as to show a wilful defiance of authority, a lawful command given personally by his superior officer in the execution of his office.'

That didn't sound like McAuslan. Unkempt, unhygienic, and unwholesome, yes, but not disobedient. Given an order, he would generally strive manfully to obey it so far as lay within his power, which wasn't far; he might forget, or fall over himself, or get lost, or start a fire, but he tried. In drink, or roused, he was unruly, admittedly, but in that case I would have expected the charge to be one of those charmingly listed under Section 10, which begins 'When concerned in a fray ...' and covers striking, offering violence, resisting an escort, and effecting an escape. But this was apparently plain, sober disobedience, which was unique.

With Bennet-Bruce away on a ski-ing course in Austria (how is it that Old Etonians get on glamorous courses like ski-ing and surf-riding, while the best I could ever manage was battle school and man management?) I was in command of the company, which involved presiding at company orders each morning, when the evil-doers of the previous day came up for judgement and slaughter. So I sat there, speculating on the new McAuslan mystery, while the Company Sergeant-Major formed up his little troupe on the veranda outside the office.

'Company ordures!' he roared – and with McAuslan involved, the mispronunciation couldn't have been more appropriate – 'Company ordures, shun! Laift tahn! Quick march, eft-ight-eft-ight-eft-ight eftwhee-ohl! Mark time!' The peaceful office was suddenly shuddering to the din of armed heels, an escort and the sweating McAuslan stamping away for dear life in front of my desk. 'Ahlt! Still!' bellowed the CSM. '14687347 Private McAuslan, J., sah!'

While the charge was read out I studied McAuslan; he was his usual dove grey colour as to the skin, and his battle dress would have disgraced a tattie-bogle. He was staring in the correct hypnotized manner over my head, standing at what he fondly believed was attention, stiffly inclined forward with his fingers crooked like a Western gunfighter. He didn't, I noticed, look particularly worried, which was unusual, for McAuslan's normal attitude to authority was one of horrified alarm. He looked almost pugnacious this morning.

'Corporal Baxter's charge, sir,' said the CSM, and Corporal Baxter stood forth. He was young and moustached and very keen.

'Sah!' exclaimed he. 'At Redford, on the 14th of this month, I was engaged in detailin' men, for the forthcomin' regimental sports, for duties, in connexion, with said sports. I placed the accused on a detail, and he refused to go. I warned him, and he still refused. I charged him, an' he became offensive. Sah!'

He saluted and stepped back. 'Well, McAuslan?' I said.

McAuslan swallowed noisily. 'He detailed me forra pilla-fight, sir.'

'The what?'

'Ra pilla-fight.'

It dawned. At the regimental sports one of the highlights was always the pillow-fight, in which contestants armed with pillows sat astride a greasy pole set over a huge canvas tank full of water. They swatted each other until one fell in.

'Corporal Baxter told you to enter for the pillow-fight?'

'Yessir. It wisnae that, but. It was whit he said – that Ah needed a damned good wash, an' that way Ah would get one.'

Some things need no great explanation. This one was clear in an instant. McAuslan, the insanitary soldier, on being taunted by the spruce young corporal, had suddenly rebelled; what had probably started off as a mocking joke on Baxter's part had suddenly become a formal order, and the enraged McAuslan had refused it. I could almost hear the exchanges.

But it was fairly ticklish. Young soldiers, recruits, are used to being 'detailed' for practically everything. Told to enter for sports, or read Gibbon's *Decline and Fall*, or learn the words of *To a Mouse*, they will do these things. As they get older they get a clearer idea of what is, and is not, a legitimate order. But the margin is difficult to define. The wise NCO doesn't give off-beat orders unless he is positive they will be obeyed, and Baxter was a fairly new corporal.

One thing was certain; McAuslan wasn't a new private. He might still be as backward as the rawest recruit, but he had heard the pipes at Alamein and had advanced, in his own disorderly fashion, to defeat Rommel. (God help the German who got in his way, I thought, for I'll bet his bayonet was rusty.) And Baxter's order should not have been given to him, and he felt outraged by it. Thoughtless and zealous people like Baxter probably didn't realize that McAuslan could feel outraged, of course.

When in doubt, grasp the essential. 'You did disobey the order?' I said.

'It wisnae fair. Ah'm no' dirty.' He said it without special defiance.

'That's not the point, McAuslan,' I said. 'You disobeyed the order.'

'Aye.' He paused. 'But he had nae — business tae talk tae me like that.'

'Look, McAuslan,' I said, 'you've been talked to that way before. We all have, it's part of the business. If you don't like it you can make a formal complaint. But you can't disobey orders, see? So I'm going to admonish you.' Privately, I was going to eat big lumps out of the officious Corporal Baxter too, but for the sake of discipline McAuslan wasn't going to know that. 'All right, Sergeant-Major.'

'Ah'm no' takin' that, sir,' said McAuslan, unexpectedly. 'Ah mean . . . Ah'm sorry, like . . . but Ah don't see why Ah should be admonished. He shouldnae hiv spoke tae me that way.' You could have heard a pin drop. For a minute he had me baffled, and then I recovered.

'You're admonished,' I said. 'For disobedience, which is a serious offence. Think yourself lucky.'

'Ah'm no' bein' admonished, sir,' he said. 'Ah want tae see the CO.'

'Oh, don't be so bloody silly,' I said. 'You don't want anything of the sort.'

'Ah do, sir. Ah'm no' bein' called dirty.'

'You are dirty,' interposed the sergeant-major. 'Look at ye.'

'Ah'm no'!' shouted McAuslan, all sense of discipline gone.

'Quiet!' I said. 'Now, look, McAuslan. Forget it. This is just nonsense. Everyone has been called dirty, some time or other. You have, I have, probably the sergeant-major has. There's nothing personal about it. We all have.'

'No' as often as I have,' said McAuslan, martyred.

'Well, you must admit that your appearance is sometimes . . . well, a bit casual. But that has nothing to do with the charge, don't you see?'

'Ah'm no hivin' it,' chanted McAuslan. 'Ah'm no' dirty.'

'Yes, y'are,' shouted the CSM. 'Be silent, ye thing!'

'Ah'm no'.'

'Shut up, McAuslan! Sergeant-Major, get him out of here!'

'Ah'm no' dirty! Ah'm as clean as onybody. Ah'm as clean as Baxter . . .'

'Don't youse dare talk tae me like that,' cried the enraged Baxter.

'Ah am. Ah am so. Ah'm no' dirty . . .'

'Dammit!' I shouted. 'This is a company office, not a jungle! Get him out of here, Sergeant-Major!'

The CSM more or less blasted McAuslan out of the room by sheer lung-power, and I heard the procession stamp away along the veranda, to a constant roar of 'Eft-ight-eft!' punctuated by a dying wail of 'Ah'm no' dirty'. The nuts, the eccentrics, I thought, I get them every time. McAuslan sensitive of abuse was certainly a new one.

Five minutes later I had forgotten about it, but then the sergeant-major was back, wearing an outraged expression. McAuslan, he said, was refusing to be admonished. He was demanding to be taken before the Commanding Officer.

'He's crackers,' I said. 'Doesn't he know when he's well off?'

'He says he wants to be marched,' said the CSM. 'The hell wi' him. Let him go.'

'The CO'll murder him,' I said. We had just got our new CO, only a few days old, a rather precise, youngish man, decent enough, but very Sandhurst. The thought of his reaction to a disobedient McAuslan was daunting. 'What's got into him, anyway? He never minded being called dirty before.'

'Ach, it's young Baxter,' said the CSM. 'He's too full of himself.'

'You can see his point, mind you,' I said. 'The idea of McAuslan going into the tank in the pillow-fight isn't unreasonable. Oh, well, there it is. See that he's at CO's orders at eleven.'

This is the Army's procedure. If an accused man isn't satisfied with the justice he gets at the lowest level, he simply demands to be 'marched' to the next higher level, in this case the battalion commander. And so on up, if he feels like it, until he gets to the House of Lords, I suppose. I had a vision of McAuslan at Westminster, facing the Woolsack and crying: 'Ah'm no' dirty,' and their Lordships intoning their verdicts, 'Dirty, upon my honour.' Not, as I had pointed out, that his cleanliness was strictly relevant to the charge of disobedience.

McAuslan's meeting with the CO was brief and sensational. Watching it, I felt like one witnessing the introduction of an orang-utan to T. Petronius Arbiter; McAuslan shambled in with his escort, the CO shivered a little as though he didn't believe it, and if he had produced a gilded pomander and swung it under his nostrils I wouldn't have been surprised.

The evidence was called again, McAuslan's refusal to be dealt with at company level was verified, the CO sighed, tucked his handkerchief into his sleeve, and asked if accused had anything to say. Accused said, predictably, that he wasn't dirty. The CO, equally predictably, said that had nothing to do with it, and that he found the case proved. He then asked, according to formula:

'Will you accept my award or go before a court-martial?' expecting the invariable acceptance. But he didn't get it. McAuslan, by this time grey with fright – the awful majesty of the CO's office quite as much as the prospect of what lay ahead must have been working on him – swayed slightly at attention, coughed horribly, rolled his eyes and closed them, and whispered hoarsely:

'Ah wannae be court-martialled, sir, thank ye.'

The CO said, 'Good God,' and asked him to repeat him-

self. McAuslan did, and there was a long silence. You could
see what the trouble was: the CO didn't want a man going
for court-martial in the first week of his command; on the
other hand, he was new, and felt he must play it by the
book. Our old Colonel, full of sin and experience, would
have sorted it out, either by terrorizing McAuslan or by
playing his celebrated let-me-be-your-father role and more
or less charming the accused into taking seven days con-
finement to barracks. But the new CO was uncertain and
on his dignity; he made some effort to find out what was
behind McAuslan's determination, but he didn't understand
his man, and his austerity of manner froze McAuslan into
dumb panic.

Finally the CO said very well, march him out, sergeant-
major, and that was McAuslan for the big time, the Bloody
Assize, the works. I don't suppose he himself had more
than a vague idea what a court-martial was, and he was
obviously incapable of understanding the difference between the matter of his plain disobedience (which he admitted) and the matter of Baxter's alleged provocation. All
he knew was that he wasn't going to be punished for his
resentment at being called dirty by a young corporal with
half his service.

At any other time, I believe, there might have been un-
official representations to the CO to clear the thing up, but
everyone was too busy. Royalty was still at Holyrood, and
within the week the Highland Division Games were due
to take place. This had not happened on a full scale since
time immemorial, for it is difficult to get all six Highland
Regiments together at one time (there being an official tendency to keep the savages apart in case they start another
'45 rebellion, or destroy each other, which is more likely).
Any Highland Games is a spectacular show, but with a full
muster of the regiments in Scotland this was expected to
be something special. Apart from the normal track and field
events which you get at any athletics meeting, there would
be such esoteric contests as throwing the hammer, tossing

the caber, Highland dancing, and piping; the tug-of-war, and the pillow-fight for which McAuslan had fastidiously refused to enter, would be the final events before the prizes were presented by one of the Royal Duchesses. Altogether it was big military, sporting, and social stuff, and McAuslan's court-martial was back-page news by comparison.

As battalion sports officer I hardly even had time to sleep; I was running myself in the quarter-mile and the relay, and I had to supervise the training of the regiment's athletes. This did not consist so much of giving them psychological pep-talks and tips on sprinting, as of keeping Wee Wullie out of the guardroom, for he was anchor man and mainstay of the tug-of-war team, and he was drinking more than usual to drown his sorrows over the old Colonel's departure. We had a pretty fair team, all round; we would hold our own in piping and dancing, would probably win the relay and certainly take the high jump, for the adjutant was a possible Olympic prospect, and we would make a respectable showing in everything else.

So it wasn't the business of making a good show in the actual competiton that worried me, so much as ensuring that our entry remained sober and of sound mind, and did nothing to disgrace the regiment's fair name. With royalty present you can't be too careful, and with competitors who have knavery and mischief running thick in their blood you have to be doubly on guard. To give just one example, I uncovered the germ of a plot – just an idea, really, it hadn't got to the blueprint stage – which involved getting hold of the caber in advance and soaking it in water. A caber is several yards of tree trunk which the competitor, a man of iron muscle invariably, must throw end over end; soaked in water it becomes so heavy as to be unmanageable, and there were those in our battalion so lost to shame as to consider it a splendid idea to doctor the caber before the Argylls or the Highland Light Infantry entrants tried to throw it. It wasn't a bad scheme, at that, but the snag was how to arrange matters so that we got the use of an unsoaked caber first. They were working on this when I got wind of it and spoiled everything by threatening disciplinary action. Anyway, as I pointed out, it was too risky.

Then there was the pipe-sergeant to soothe and quieten. He was alarmed to distraction because the adjutant 'iss participating in the godless high chump, Mr MacNeill, sir, when I want him for the foursome. Look yonder,' he cried, 'at him hurling himself over a silly bit stick when he should be at the dancing, with a one-two. He will injure himself, and I'll be left with Corporal Cattenach that has no more sense of the time than a Hawick farmer. Can you not appeal to him, sir?'

'He can win the high jump and dance in your foursome, too, pipey,' I said.

'Aye, can he, and if he strains himself, with ruptures and torn ligaments, where are we?' cried the pipey. 'Which is the more important for a Highland Games, the fine dancing or . . . or yon abomination? Any clown can loup, sir, but the dear Adjutant is a dancer in ten thousand, see the grace of him. Ach, damn,' he added petulantly, 'they have spoiled all decent sport with their bluidy athletics!'

I left him lamenting, and spent half an hour with our juvenile entry, for the Games included children's sports, and our regimental infants were toiling busily in preparation for the three-legged race, the bean bag, the bunny jump, and the under-ten eighty-yard dash. In this last we were strong, for we had the twin sons of Corporal Coupar, known locally as the Bullet-headed Little Bandits. They were wicked, fearless, malevolent-looking urchins of nine, infamous for their evil-doing and their language, which would have earned censure in a Tollcross pub. But they could run; years of evading the wrath of regimental cooks, their father, and those private soldiers who were sensitive to juvenile abuse had made them faster than chain lightning with a link snapped. Barring accidents, the eighty-yard dash was ours. I seized one twin as he shot by, and received a hair-curling rebuke.

'Don't use that disgusting word,' I said. 'Are you Davie or Donnie?'

'Name o' the wee man,' said he. 'Can ye no' tell? Ah'm Donnie. Ah don't look like that, surely?' And he indicated his twin with distaste. Davie retorted, unmentionably.

'David!' I beckoned him, and he came defiantly. 'Now, look, both of you. Do you want any more stories?'

The two small, ugly faces looked slightly concerned. They liked their stories.

'Right,' I said. 'Unless you cut out swearing, no more stories. You should be ashamed. What would your father say?'

Dave sniggered. 'Ye should hear him.'

I slapped him on his trouser seat. 'Don't be impertinent. And what's more, I won't let you run in the sports. Yes, I thought that would worry you. Anyway, are you going to win?'

'No kiddin',' said Donnie scornfully. 'We'll dawdle it.'

'Ye mean Ah'll dawdle it,' said Davie.

'You? You couldnae catch me in a bus.'

'Could Ah no'? You couldnae run wi' the cold.'

I rolled them on the ground briefly, which one should always do to small boys, and was preparing to go on my way when Davie picked himself up from the grass and called :

'Hey, Mr MacNeill. Is it right McAuslan's goin' tae get the jail?'

This stopped me short. 'What do you know about it?'

'Ah heard my daddy sayin' McAuslan had had it. Is that right?'

'I don't know,' I said. 'Why are you interested?'

'Och,' said Davie. 'Ah like McAuslan. He's that — dirty.'

'Ah hate Corporal Baxter,' said Donnie viciously. 'He's a —'

I despaired. You might as well have tried to stop an alcoholic tippling as purify the conversation of the Bullet-headed Little Bandits. Oddly enough, though, I felt sympathy for both their views, and in the next few days, while the athletes trained and the pipers practised, and the wooden grandstands were erected and the tents pitched and all was made ready for the Games, I found McAuslan increasingly on my mind. The Games were on Friday and Saturday, and McAuslan's trial was fixed for the Friday afternoon. He looked like a dead duck, and I wondered how stiff a sentence he would get. Disobeying an order may be admonished at company level, but when it gets before a court-martial it can be a detention offence, quite easily, and McAuslan doing twenty-one days in the iron discipline of a glasshouse was a worrying thought. He wasn't exactly cut out for doing everything at the double and in spotless order.

His defending officer, the 'prisoner's friend', arrived on the Wednesday afternoon. He was a thin, nervous Cockney Jew, with a hard-worn captain's uniform and enormous horn-rimmed spectacles. His other distinguishing characteristics were a huge Adam's apple, a blue lantern jaw, a pendulous nose, and an unhappy expression.

'Name of Einstein,' he said, shaking hands limply. 'Don't make any mathematical jokes, for God's sake, I couldn't stand it. No kidding, I'm thinking of changing it to Shylock.' He laid his battered briefcase on my desk and sank into a chair, massaging his forehead. 'Honest, I've just about had it. Had to stand all the way from York. I'm bushed. Usual last-minute flap, of course. You think you've got it tough in the infantry, mate, you ought to see the Army's bloody legal department. To give you an idea,' – he removed his glasses and stared at me with great spaniel eyes – 'I still don't know the first thing about this ruddy case; not a thing! Organization! Oh, they did give me the documents, but I seem to have left 'em somewhere. I should cocoa. As my old man said, "Any lawyer that needs a brief needs a bloody nursemaid". And he was no mug, my old man. What's the charge?'

'Disobeying an order,' I said, and he looked surprised.

'Bit of a come-down for your lot, isn't it? I mean to say, last time I was mixed up with a Highland mob it was murder, arson, and making away with Government property in the face of the enemy. Disobedience, eh? Well, it's a living. And as my old man so wisely said, bless his black heart, "Always be happy to do business with the Gentile Tribe, Frankie, you may need a free kilt some day".' His vulpine face assumed a friendly beam. 'So just fill me in, old man, would you?'

I told him the McAuslan saga, pillow-fight, new CO, objection to being called dirty, and all, and he sat sucking his teeth and twitching.

'Well, some mothers do have them,' he observed when I had finished. 'Got a fag on you, old man?'

I lit him up and asked him how long he thought McAuslan would get.

'Get?' he said, staring at me through the smoke. 'Whaddya mean, "get"?'

'Well, he doesn't seem to have much chance—'

'Not much chance? Don't make me laugh. He's going to get acquitted, mate, don't you worry about that. All my clients get acquitted. There's more of my clients walking about free men than you've had hot dinners. "Get" forsooth! I like that.'

'I'm sorry, I—'

'What we've got to decide on,' said Einstein, waving me to silence, 'is a line of defence. Yers-ss. Let's see . . . How about steady-responsible-hard-working-soldier-victimized-by-cruel-superior? Old, but sound.'

'No, not with McAuslan . . . I don't think . . .'

'Just an idea,' he shrugged. 'Wait, I've got a good one. How about religious-fanatic-wounded-in-his-beliefs? That's a beauty. Show a court a holy man and they get the willies every time.'

'McAuslan isn't holy,' I said. 'He's probably an atheist.'

'You're not helping, you know,' said Einstein severely.

'Tell you what, is he deaf? No? It's never much good, anyway. I don't suppose he's illegitimate, either?'

'Illegitimate?'

'A bastard, you know,' he explained patiently. ''Cos if he was, and this corporal called him one, it'd be a lovely extenuating circumstance. I used that one once, out in Port Sudan. Gift from the gods. President of the court turned out to be a bastard himself. Turned a certain two years for mutinous behaviour into a straight acquittal.' He chuckled reminiscently. 'Those were the days, mate, those were the days.'

'Well, this is today,' I said with some heat, for it seemed to me Captain Einstein was approaching things in a decidedly offhand manner. 'And McAuslan . . .'

'I know, I know,' he flapped his hands at me. 'I'm just exploring, see? Getting the feel of things, looking for a line.' He meditated. 'He isn't normal and steady, he isn't religious, he isn't deaf, and he isn't a bastard. What the hell is he, a cave-man?'

'You said it, not me.'

'Oh.' He stared at me. 'Well. In that case, maybe I'd better have a little talk with him.' He slapped his pockets. 'I say, got another fag on you? I seem to have left mine . . . Ta. Yes, I'll have to reorientate a bit, I can see. To quote my old man again, "If you can't find a good line of defence, just stick to the truth". Let's go and interview the body.'

When he saw McAuslan, who was sitting on his bunk in the cells, looking foul and miserable, Einstein had a quick intake of breath, most of it cigarette smoke, and a coughing fit.

'Gawd,' he said reverently, when he had recovered. 'You don't half pick 'em, don't you? He looks like a distressed area. I can see I'm going to have to be at my talented smoothest to make *him* look good in court. Oh, well, never say die, all things are possible. I mean to say, if you've got a Church of England chaplain off on an embezzlement charge, you can do practically anything, can't you? I've done that, too. Tell you what,' he added, laying a hand on my shoulder, 'why don't you buzz off to the mess and get some drink set up while I have a word with old Private Piltdown here? See you in ten minutes.' He winked. 'And don't look so worried, old cock. Your boy is in capable hands, believe me.'

I hoped sincerely that he was right, this voluble Einstein, but I'd have been happier if he had looked just a bit less of a villain. Frankly, when it came to appearances, I'd sooner have been represented by Blackbeard Teach.

Nor did he seem terribly energetic. Having spent only ten minutes with McAuslan, he came to the mess and drank me nearly bankrupt, ate a hearty dinner, and then took seven and six off the MO at snooker. The following day he passed in loafing about the barracks, having a word here and there, returning frequently to the mess to hit the Glenfiddich, and generally looking like a man without a care in the world. I didn't know how legal men prepared for mortal combat, but I was pretty sure they spent more time poring over papers and hunting out surprise witnesses than swilling whisky and trying to lure people to the billiards table.

Then it was Friday morning, and I had the heats of the quarter-mile to worry about: I had modest hopes of getting into the final, and maybe picking up a point or two there. As it turned out, the thing was money for jam, thanks to Corporal Pudden and my own cleverly psychological running. I discovered as a lad that to succeed in the quarter-mile, against any but really good runners, all you have to do is to set off at top speed from the start. This discourages the mob, who think you must be good; they tend to take it easy in consequence, and by the time they realize their mistake, when you are wheezing and reeling through the last hundred yards, it is probably too late for them to make up lost ground.

So when my heat lined up – Pudden and I were the only representatives of our regiment – and the gun barked, I went off like the clappers. As far as the back straight I was doing fine, but by three-quarters of the way round my evil living – cigarettes, marshmallows, and the like – was taking its toll, and by the time I hit the straight I was giving a fair imitation of the last survivor staggering into the garrison, weak with loss of blood. However, unknown to me, Corporal Pudden, who couldn't run particularly well, but was broad in the beam, had established himself in second place, and by judicious weaving across the track was preventing the opposition from getting past. This enabled me to get home by a comfortable margin, and Pudden, having body-checked a Seaforth who was trying to take the long way round him, just nosed out a Highland Light Infantryman for second place. So after that there was really nothing to do except put my tunic on over my strip and lounge about looking professional, watching the other heats, slapping my calves thoughtfully, and generally behaving like a man to whom both heats and finals are just formalities.

Friday morning, of course, was just the weeding out; the big stuff, finals and so on, was for next day. They were still putting up the last marquees and making a kind of royal box with red carpet when I went off to have lunch, change into my best uniform, and present myself at the opening of McAuslan's court-martial.

It was held in a big, bare room somewhere in Redford Barracks, and such are memory's tricks that I can remember nothing more of the background than that. There was a long plain table for the members of the court, the president of which was a sad-looking Sapper colonel with bags under his eyes. There was a square, tough-looking major in the Devons, and a very pink young man with chain epaulettes on his shoulders – a cavalryman of sorts. There was also a prosecutor, tall and lean and (to me) looking full of malevolence and brains; there was Einstein, nervous and rather untidy, muttering to himself and diving in and out of his briefcase; he saw me sitting on the chairs for witnesses and spectators, and came over confidentially.

'Bit of a break gettin' an engineer for president,' he whispered. 'They're all barmy. Can't say I like the look of that major from the Bloody Eleventh, though; he'll be a martinet, no error. Dunno about the boy; that type you can never tell – might be soft-hearted, might be a sadist. Think we could risk a fag? No, better not. Bad impression.' He removed his glasses, fidgeted, and drew my attention to Prosecution. 'One of the worst, I'd say; you know, the Middle - Temple - if - it - please - your - ludship - my - pater - was-a-KC type. Creeps, the lot o' them.'

'How's McAuslan?' I asked.

'Clean,' said Einstein, 'thanks to the efforts of a couple of lads who've been scrubbing him half the morning. I told the brute straight, I said, "You may be guilty, but by God, at least you're going to look innocent." They just took him to the showers and went at him with brushes; shifted a power of dirt, they did. Hallo, curtain up.' There was a thump of marching boots outside. Einstein slid out of his seat. 'Well, into thy hands, Blind Justice, and may God defend the right, or something,' he muttered, and went back to his table.

There was a roar of commands, a stamping on the polished boards, and in came prisoner and escort, marching like crazy. McAuslan was in somebody's best tunic and tartan – certainly not his own – and for the first time in my experience his face was pink, not grey. Whoever had washed him had done a terrific job; he looked like a normal human being – well, nearly normal, for his habit of swinging leg and arm together was still apparent, and when he halted he crouched at attention rather than stood. But his hair appeared to have been stuck down with glue, and when he sat, trembling violently, in the accused's chair, he looked much as any other court-martial candidate looks – scared and lonely, but not scruffy.

There is something frighteningly simple about a court-martial. It is justice stripped to the bare essentials. Usually only prosecutor and prisoner's friend have any legal knowledge; for the rest it is common sense backed by King's

Regulations and the Army Act. There is a minimum of ceremony, and for that matter a minimum of talk. But it is
probably the fairest shake in the world.

The charge was read, and Einstein pleaded not guilty.
The president nodded mournfully to Prosecution, who got
up and began to deliver himself, outlining the case against
the accused in a languid, matter-of-fact Oxford accent.

The impression he gave was that Corporal Baxter, an
NCO of sterling character and charming disposition, had
approached McAuslan and suggested that he enter for the
inter-regimental pillow-fight. McAuslan, laughing such a
laugh as the pious might conceive on the lips of Satan, had
refused in the most savage terms. Corporal Baxter, disappointed rather than annoyed, had pleaded with him win-
ningly; McAuslan had repeated his refusal and added the
foulest abuse. In spite of this, Corporal Baxter had per-
severed with forebearing firmness, but the hardened scoun-
drel would not be moved, and eventually, with great
reluctance, Baxter had put him on a charge. Thereupon
McAuslan had offered him the vilest threats, which might
well have been taken as the prelude to an assault. No
assault had taken place, admittedly, but Prosecution obviously thought it had been a close thing. He then called
Corporal Baxter.

Hearing it the way Prosecution had told it, I could see
McAuslan already on the rockpile; there seemed no possible
defence, and I was surprised to see Einstein looking bored
and inattentive. I knew very little about courts.

Corporal Baxter strode masterfully in, looking slightly
pale and young, with his stripes gleaming whitely, and took
the oath. In more formal language he repeated what Prosecution had said.

'Let us be quite clear, Corporal,' said Prosecution suavely,
when Baxter had finished. 'You ordered the accused to enter for this event, the pillow-fight. What words did you
use, so well as you can recall?'

'I remember exactly, sir,' said Baxter confidently. 'I said,

"You'll put your name down for the pillow-fight, Mc-Auslan".'

'I see. And he said?'

'He said he bloody well wouldn't, sir.'

'Very good. And after you had repeated the order, and again he refused, you charged him, and he became abusive?'

'Yessir.'

'What did he say?'

Baxter hesitated. 'He called me a shilpit wee nyaff, sir.'

The president stirred. 'He called you what?'

Baxter coloured slightly. 'A shilpit wee nyaff.'

The president looked at Prosecution. 'Perhaps you can translate?'

Prosecution, hand it to him, didn't even blink. He selected a paper from his table, held it up at arm's length, and said gravely:

'Shilpit, I am informed, sir, signifies stunted, undergrown. As to "wee", that is, of course, current in English as well as in . . .' he paused for a second '. . . the Northern dialects. Nyaff, an insignificant person, a pip-squeak.'

'Remarkable,' said the president. 'Nyaff. Ny-ahff.' He tried it round his tongue. 'Expressive. Synonymous with the Norse "niddering".'

'Sir?' said Prosecution.

'Niddering,' said the president. 'A worthless person, a nonentity. Possibly a connexion there. So many of these Norse pejoratives begin with "n".'

Einstein coughed slightly. 'Hebrew, too, sir. "Nebbish" means much the same thing.'

'Indeed?' The president brightened. 'I'm obliged to you. Nyaff,' he repeated with satisfaction. 'Remarkable. Do go on.'

Prosecution, looking slightly rattled, turned again to Baxter.

'And after he had called you . . . these names?'

'He called me a glaikit sumph.'

You could see Prosecution wishing he hadn't asked. The

president was looking hopeful. 'Sumph,' said the president with relish. 'That's strong.' He looked inquiring, and Prosecution sighed.

'Sumph, a dullard, an uninspired person, a stick-in-the-mud. Glaikit, loose-jointed, awkward, ill-formed.' He put down his paper with resignation. 'There is more, sir, in the dialect and in ordinary speech, but I question whether . . ."

'What else did he call you?' said the president, taking control. Baxter looked sulky.

'A rotten big bastard,' he said.

'Oh.' The president looked disappointed. He shot a glance at McAuslan, as though he had hoped for better things. 'All right, then. Carry on, please.'

The major suddenly intervened. 'This was just common abuse?'

'Pretty uncommon, I should say,' observed the young cavalryman cheerfully.

Prosecution, obviously deciding that things must be put on the right lines again, addressed Baxter :

'Common abuse or not, the point is that a definite order, clearly given and understood, was disobeyed. You are quite clear on that?'

'Yes, sir.' You could see that Baxter didn't care for courts-martial. They just exposed him to a repetition of unpleasant personalities. 'I gave him a good chance, sir, but he just kept refusin'.'

Unbelievably, McAuslan spoke. 'Ah called him a two-strippit git, as weel,' he announced.

This produced an immediate sensation in court. Prosecution rounded indignantly on the accused, the escort snarled at him to be silent, Einstein dropped his spectacles, and the president said he hadn't caught the last word properly. McAuslan, startled at the effect of his intervention, got up hurriedly, upset his chair, cursed richly, and was thrust back into his seat by a savagely whispering regimental policeman. When order had been restored, and the president had been heard to murmur, 'Git, get, geat –

possibly Geat, a Goth. Wiglaf was a Geat, wasn't he?'
Einstein rose for cross-examination.

'Odd kind of order, wasn't it, Corporal — to enter for a
pillow-fight?'

'I was detailing men for duties connected wi' the sports,'
said Baxter stiffly.

'What other events did you order people to enter?' asked
Einstein.

Baxter hesitated. 'The others I ordered were for fatigues,
like settin' up hurdles and helpin' wi' the tents.'

'I see. And why did you order the prisoner into the
pillow-fight? Why him, particularly?'

Baxter looked sullen, and Einstein repeated his question.
'This was the only soldier you ordered to enter a specific
event. Now, why him, and why the pillow-fight?'

'He was dirty, sir, and I told him he could do wi' a
wash.'

'Dirty, was he? Had he been on fatigues?'

'He's always dirty,' said Baxter firmly.

'Oh, he hadn't been on fatigues? You're sure of that?'

'Well, yes, sir,' said Baxter. 'He had been on fatigues . . .'

'What fatigues?' snapped Einstein.

'Ablutions, sir.'

'So he had every right to be dirty at that time?'

'Yes, sir, but . . .'

'Never mind "but". If he was dirty then, it was only
natural, considering the fatigues he had been doing, isn't
that so?'

'He's always dirty, sir,' insisted Baxter. 'He's the dirtiest
thing in the battalion . . .'

'Stand up, prisoner,' said Einstein. 'Now, Corporal, take
a good look at him, and tell me : is he dirty?'

Baxter looked at McAuslan, balefully. 'Ye wouldnae expect him to be . . .'

'Answer my question! Is he dirty?'

'No, sir.'

'Yet you said he was *always* dirty. Well, Corporal?'

'It's the first time I've seen him clean,' said Baxter doggedly.

'Ye're a bloody liar,' said McAuslan, aggrieved.

'Ah'm no' . . .'

There were further sensations at this, culminating in a stern warning to the prisoner – I doubt if it would have been half as stern if he had employed a choice Caledonian epithet instead of Anglo-Saxon which the president knew already. Then Einstein resumed, on a different tack.

'When you gave this alleged order, Corporal . . .'

'I can't have that,' said Prosecution rising. 'Defence's use of the word alleged is calculated to throw doubt on the witness's veracity, which is not in question.'

'Who says it's not?' demanded Einstein. 'He's admitted one mis-statement already.'

'He has done no such thing. That is deliberately to distort his evidence. I submit . . .'

'Perhaps we could rephrase the question?' suggested the president, back to his normal despondent self now that there were no further fine avenues to explore in McAuslan's vocabulary.

'Very good, sir,' said Einstein. 'Corporal, before you gave the order which you've told us you gave, did you not *suggest*, as distinct from ordering, to the accused that he enter the pillow-fight?'

'It was an order, sir,' said Baxter.

'But wasn't it given, well, jocularly, in fun, you know?'

Cunning Einstein knew quite well that if he could get even a hint of admission on this point, he had put a big nail in the prosecution's case. But not-so-cunning Baxter knew that much too.

'No, sir,' he said stoutly.

'No smile? No – well, you know – no case of, "Hey soldier, you look pretty mucky; how about getting a good wash in the pillow-fight?" Wasn't that it? And didn't the prisoner treat it as a joke, and tell you, joking in turn, to get lost? Wasn't that about it, Corporal?'

'No, sir, it was not.'

'And didn't you take offence at this, and *turn* the joke into an order?'

'No, sir, definitely not.'

'Do you know that the prisoner claims that you *did* smile, at first, and that he didn't take your order seriously until, much to his surprise, you put him on a charge?'

'I don't know that, sir.'

'You never realized that he thought you were being funny?'

'No, sir.'

'Have you ever ordered a man to go in for a pillow-fight before?'

'No, sir.'

'Ever heard of such a thing?'

'I've heard of orders being given, sir,' said Baxter boldly.

'That wasn't my question, Corporal, and you know it. Have you ever heard of a man being ordered to enter a pillow-fight?'

'No, sir.'

'So you would agree it isn't a common order?'

'No, sir.'

'Right,' said Einstein. 'Thank you, Corporal. No more questions.'

Prosecution was actually rising when Einstein bobbed up again, as though he had forgotten something.

'I'm sorry, just one more question after all. Corporal, how long have you been a corporal?'

'Three weeks, sir.'

Einstein sat down without a word.

Prosecution contented himself with re-emphasizing that an order had been given and understood, and got Baxter to clarify the point about McAuslan's dirtiness: McAuslan, Baxter said, had always been dirty until the present occasion.

'When you would expect him to be looking his best?' asked Prosecution.

'Oh, yes, sir.'

'Thank you, Corporal. That's all.'

Baxter saluted and strode out, and Prosecution called Lance-Corporal Bakie, who corroborated Baxter's evidence as to McAuslan's refusal of a straightforward order. No, Bakie had not seen Baxter smile at any time, nor had McAuslan appeared to regard the order as anything but a serious one. In Bakie's view, the refusal had been pure badness on McAuslan's part, but then McAuslan was notoriously a bad bas . . . a bad soldier. Dirty? Oh, yes, something shocking.

Einstein didn't even bother to cross-examine, and when Bakie stood down Prosecution announced that that was it, from his side. He seemed satisfied; he had made his point clearly, it seemed to me. Einstein, muttering and rummaging through his papers, presently rose to open the defence, and to an accompaniment of crashing furniture and stifled swearing, Private McAuslan took the stand.

Looking at him, as he stood listening in evident agitation while they explained what taking the oath meant, I decided that while he was certainly clean for once, that was about all you could say for him. He looked like Sixteen-string Jack on his way to Tyburn, keenly conscious of his position.

Einstein got up, and McAuslan clung to him mentally like a monkey to its mother. Then Einstein started questioning him, slowly and gently, and to my surprise McAuslan responded well. No, he had not taken the order seriously; he had thought Baxter was at the kidding; who ever heard of a fella bein' told tae get intae a pilla-fight? In a military career that stretched from Tobruk onwards (trust Einstein) McAuslan had never heard of such a thing. Oh, aye, Baxter had been smilin'; grinnin' a' ower his face, a' the fellas in the room had seen it.

'Have you ever refused an order, McAuslan?' said Einstein.

'S'help ma Goad, no, sir. Ye can ask Mr MacNeill.'

'You realize that if you have, and been convicted of it, that may appear during this trial? In which case you know, you can be charged with perjury?'

McAuslan called the gods of Garscube Road to witness his innocence. I was pretty sure he hadn't ever been disobedient – dirty, idle, slovenly, drunk, you name it, McAuslan had been it, but probably he had never wilfully disobeyed a lawful command.

'But, look here, McAuslan,' said Einstein. 'You said some pretty rough things to the corporal, you know. We heard them. How about those?'

'That wis when he got nasty, and started sayin' Ah wis dirty,' said McAuslan vehemently. 'Ah'm no' havin' that. Ah'm no' dirty. He'd nae business tae say that.'

It sounded convincing, although I was certain Einstein had rehearsed him in it. Despite his original protestations to me and to the CO, when his rage was hot against the upstart Baxter, McAuslan must know he was generally regarded as personally fit only for the dead cart. There had been times in the past when he had seemed to take a satisfaction in his squalor; he had been forcibly washed more than once.

'So, this is your case, then.' Einstein, hands on hips, stared at the floor. 'You thought the corporal was joking, and so you didn't take his order seriously. When he said you were dirty and should enter the pillow-fight to get a wash, you resented it, but you didn't think he really meant you to enter the pillow-fight?'

'That's right, sir.'

'And then he charged you, and you swore at him.'

'Aye.'

'You aren't charged with swearing at him, of course,' Einstein was casual. 'And you contend that when Corporal Baxter says you're a dirty soldier, he is not telling the truth.'

'He's not, sir. Ah'm no' dirty. Ye can ask Mr Mac . . .'

Not if you've any sense, you won't, I thought. I'd do

a lot for McAuslan, but perjuring myself to the extent of saying he wasn't dirty would have been too much.

'Tell me, McAuslan,' said Einstein confidentially. 'The reason why you didn't take the order seriously was that you felt that it was silly and unreasonable, wasn't it? I mean, the corporal was really telling you, in a rather nasty way, to get washed. That right? And you knew that wasn't sensible. Oh, I know you'd been on ablutions, but his order implied that you were habitually filthy, didn't it? And you knew that wasn't right?'

Prosecution rose languidly. 'Really, I feel the witness is being led, rather. At this rate defence might as well give his evidence for him.'

There was a bit of legal snarling, and the president mumbled at them, and then Einstein resumed.

'Did you think such an order, given seriously, could reasonably apply to you?'

'No, sir. Ah didnae.'

God forgive you, McAuslan, I thought. Morally, I may be on your side, but legally you're a perjured ruffian. And Einstein, the clown, was making it worse.

'You take a pride in your appearance, McAuslan?'

'Yes, sir.'

Now I'd heard everything.

Einstein sat down, and Prosecution came slowly to his feet, stropping his claws. McAuslan turned to face him as if he were one of the Afrika Korps. Now, I thought, you poor disorderly soldier, you're for it, but somehow it didn't turn out that way. McAuslan knew his story, and he stuck to it: he hadn't disobeyed, he wasn't dirty. Prosecution put his questions suavely, sneeringly, angrily, and Einstein never made a murmur, but McAuslan just sat there with his ugly head lowered and said, 'No, sir,' or 'Ah didnae, sir.' Prosecution's cross-examination was falling flat; you can't play clever tricks with a witness who just persists in dogged denial, and eventually he gave it up. McAuslan went back to the accused's chair, and I felt that on balance he had made not a bad show – better than I'd expected, by a long way.

Then the blow fell. Einstein called Private Brown, who testified that Baxter had been leering wickedly, and had not intended the order seriously; not at first, anyway. Baxter thought he was good, Brown opined, and often took the mickey out of the fellas. So far so good; Brown stuck to his story under cross-examination, and then Prosecution drove his horse and cart through the middle of the defence's case.

'The court has been told that the accused didn't take the order seriously,' he informed Brown, 'and it has been implied that his reason for this attitude was that such an order couldn't apply to him. He contends – the defence will correct me if I'm wrong – that he is a clean soldier, and that therefore the order to enter the pillow-fight (and consequently get a bath) couldn't be taken seriously. What do you think of that?'

Einstein was up like a shot. 'Witness' opinion of evidence is not itself evidence.'

Prosecution bowed. 'All right. I'll change the question. Is McAuslan a clean soldier?'

Brown, who was well named Daft Bob, grinned. 'Ah widnae say that, sir.'

You could feel the court stiffen.

'You wouldn't?' Prosecution's voice was honeyed. 'What would you call him?'

Brown, realizing that this mattered, and torn between fear of the court and loyalty to one who was, after all, his comrade, hesitated.

'Ah don't know, sir.'

'Oh, yes, you do. Is he clean or not, smart or not?'

'He's no' very clean, sir.' A pause. 'We had to wash him once.'

'So his contention that he couldn't believe the order was serious is simply nonsense?'

'Ah . . . Ah suppose so, sir.'

Einstein did his best in re-examination, but it was no use. No honest witness from the battalion could have called McAuslan anything but dirty, and Einstein had made his cleanliness the keystone of the defence. Why he had, I couldn't guess, but he had cooked McAuslan all the way. Prosecution was looking serene when Daft Bob stood down, the court was looking solemn and stern, Einstein was looking worried.

There was a pause, and then the president asked if the defence had any further witnesses. Einstein looked blank for a minute, with his mouth open, said 'Errr' at some length, and then ended abruptly, 'Yessir. Yes, one more, sir.' He stood up, straightened his rumpled tunic, and called out:

'Regimental Sergeant-Major Mackintosh!'

If he had called General de Gaulle I'd have been less surprised. I couldn't think of a good reason for calling the RSM, just a few bad ones. If Einstein was hoping to get helpful evidence here, he was, as the Jocks say, away with the fairies.

The RSM came in, like Astur the great Lord of Luna, with stately stride. He was in great shape, from the glittering silver of his stag's head badge to the gloriously polished black of his boots, six and a quarter feet of kilted splendour. He crashed to a halt before the president, swept him a salute, took the oath resoundingly, kissed the book – the sheer military dignity of that one action would have won Napoleon's heart – and sat down, folding the pleats of his kilt deftly beneath him. Einstein approached him like a slightly nervous ambassador before a throne.

'You are John Mackintosh, Regimental Sergeant-Major of this battalion?'

'I am, sir.'

'I see, yes.' Having established that, Einstein seemed uncertain how to proceed. 'Er . . . tell the court, please, er . . . Mr Mackintosh – have you always been with this regiment?'

'No, sir,' said the RSM. 'Having completed my early service in this regiment, I was for twelve years in the Brigade of Guards. The Scots Guards, to be exact.'

'Thank you,' said Einstein. 'May I ask what rank you attained – in the Guards?'

'Drill Sergeant, sir. I served in that capacity at the Pirbright depot.'

Which is to say that Mackintosh had been one of the two or three smartest and most expert parade-ground soldiers in the world. It didn't surprise me.

'And after that?'

'I was attached to the Second Commando durin' the late war, sir, before returnin' to the Scots Guards in 1943. Shortly afterwards I was transferred to this battalion.'

'As RSM?'

'In my present capacity, sir; yes.'

Which rounded off his military service nicely, but hadn't done much to clear up the case of Rex v. McAuslan. Einstein was scratching himself; Prosecution was looking slightly amused.

'Tell me, Mr Mackintosh,' said Einstein. 'Having served in the Guards, as you've told us, would you say . . . well, would you disagree, if I said you were probably a leading authority on military standards and deportment?'

The RSM considered this, sitting upright like a Caesar, one immaculate hose-topped leg thrust forward, hand on knee. He permitted himself a half-smile.

'I would not disagree, sir – no. But if there is any credit in that, it belongs entirely to the Guards, and to my present regiment.'

'Well, that's very nicely put,' said Einstein. 'However, I think we'd all agree that you are an expert in that field.'

Go on, I thought, ask him what he thinks of McAuslan; let's really go out with a bang, so that we can all whimper later.

'What is your opinion,' said Einstein carefully, 'of the standard of drill and dress in this battalion?'

'It is high, sir,' said the RSM.

'You've seen to that?'

'Not I alone, sir. I believe I can say, with some confidence, that the battalion will bear comparison wi' any in Scotland, or wi' any regiment of the Line.'

'With the Guards?' asked Einstein mischievously.

'Hardly that, sir.' The RSM gave another of his paternal half-smiles. 'Capability of smartness,' he went on impressively, 'is a pre-requis-ite of a Guardsman. This is not so in a Highland regiment, to the same extent. We do nott handpick for size, for example. But I would have not the slightest quaahlms, sirr, in matchin' this battalion, for turn-oot and drill, wi' any in the worrld outside the Brigade.'

'I'm sure you wouldn't,' said Einstein, pleasantly. 'I think, in fact, if I remember rightly, that this battalion recently provided a very special honour guard for a royal occasion, didn't it? Which would bear out what you've been telling us?'

'You're referring, sir, to the guard-mounting at Edinburgh Castle? Yes, the battalion provided the guard for that occasion.' The RSM glanced in my direction. 'Mr MacNeill there, was in charge of the guard-mountin'. With myself, of course.'

Then it hit me. I saw where Einstein was going, and it froze my marrow. Oh, yes, the RSM and I had been there, and we weren't the only ones.

'Of course,' Einstein was continuing. 'It was a very responsible occasion, I imagine, for both of you. On such occasions, Mr Mackintosh, I imagine that really extra-special care is taken with the guard – with its appearance, turn-out, and so on?'

'Naturally so, sir.'

'The battalion will give of its very best, in fact – in drill, turn-out, and so forth?'

'Yes, sir.' There was a slight frown on the RSM's face; he was wondering why Einstein was hammering so obvious a point.

'But of course, that's a question of the men involved, isn't it? That's what it boils down to – you put your best men on to a guard like that. In front of royalty, I mean, only the best will do, won't it?'

Still frowning, the RSM said, 'I think that is quite obvious, sir.'

'Good,' said Einstein happily. 'I'm glad you agree. Tell me, Mr Mackintosh: do you see anyone in this room who was a member of that guard of honour? That very special guard on which, as you've told us, only the very smartest and best in the battalion would do?'

The RSM had once stopped a burst from a German mortar; I doubt if it hit him harder than the implication of what he had been saying when he digested the question, surveyed the room, and saw McAuslan – McAuslan who, although he was the central figure of the trial, hadn't been referred to since the RSM entered the room, and whom Mackintosh had naturally not connected with all the questions about smartness and turn-out and the battalion's standards. But if he had been slow before, the RSM was fast enough to see now how he had been hooked. Perhaps he blinked, but that was all.

'Do you see anyone of that guard, Mr Mackintosh?' Einstein repeated gently.

'The accused,' said the RSM, looking at McAuslan as though he was Hamlet's father. 'I see Private McAuslan.'

There was a sharp intake of breath from one of the court; all three of them stiffened.

'The accused,' repeated Einstein slowly, 'was a member of that guard, which consists, I think, of five private soldiers apart from NCOs. Five men out of a battalion of – how many?'

'Seven hundred and forty-six on parade strength, sir, thirty-two on leave, five sick, eleven on courses...'

'Quite, quite,' interrupted Einstein. 'We get the point.' He sighed and took off his glasses. 'So when five private soldiers were needed for the most important ceremonial

occasion – a royal occasion – that your battalion has parti-
cipated in since the war, I dare say, when smartness, appearance,' – he paused – 'and cleanliness are all-important
– McAuslan was one of the five on parade?'

Nicely put, you had to admit it.

'Yes, sir,' said the RSM, slowly.

'Thank you, Mr Mackintosh, no more questions,' said
Einstein, and sat down. I was too scared to look at Prosecution. Let him bound to his feet now and ask Mackintosh
his opinion of McAuslan's bodily condition, and the RSM
was caught between perjury and ridicule. And not only he;
the battalion could have been made to look a laughing-
stock. But Prosecution, when I dared to look, was plainly
too bewildered to think quickly enough, and Mackintosh
knew better than to give him a chance. The RSM rose, as
though that was all, crashed his foot on the boards, gave
the court a look that commanded dismissal if ever a look
did, saluted, turned about, and strode majestically from
the room. Prosecution made no attempt to have him
stopped; either he was too shaken by the RSM's bombshell,
or he simply didn't think it worth while cross-examining.
At any rate he just sat there, looking slightly peeved, while
the RSM strode out (only Einstein and I knew he was running away, for the first time in his life). The door closed.

After that the president called for closing addresses, and
Prosecution got slowly to his feet and repeated the order-
was-clearly-given-and-disobeyed line; it sounded lame, but
it was all he could do. Then Einstein got up and laid about
him. It was fine, impassioned stuff which left the impression that McAuslan was the RSM's admired and special
favourite, doted upon for his salubrious brilliance and perfect cleanliness. How could this model soldier, this paragon
who had been specially selected for the guard of honour (I
tried not to remember the true circumstances) be represented – as the prosecution had tried to represent him – as
noisome and unseemly? Plainly, Einstein asserted, Corporal

Baxter was mistaken, to say the least of it. Plainly, McAuslan was entitled to think that he was being jested with when he was told to enter the pillow-fight and get washed. His personal cleanliness, which was the crux of the whole affair, had just been demonstrated in the most convincing manner, by a highly senior warrant officer who judged by the standards of the Brigade of Guards. And so on. It would have made you weep; it really would.

The court was out for less than twenty minutes. They found McAuslan not guilty.

'Key witness at the last minute,' said Einstein to me as he shovelled his papers away. 'Never fails. And why? Let me tell you, mate. Courts-martial are human, unlike judges; they like you to make their flesh creep; they want you to slip the ace down your sleeve just when all is lost. "Make 'em feel warm and clever, son, and you'll sit on the Woolsack yet," my dear old dad used to say. Mind you, that RSM of yours is a bloody jewel, he really is. Perfect witness. Ah well,' he buckled his briefcase up, 'that's show business. See you in court, old man.'

It is a matter of record that Private McAuslan, on realizing that he was not going to be shot, shambled straight from the court to the battalion sports office and there entered for the inter-regimental pillow-fight. He was not going to have it supposed, he explained, that he was feart. Far from it; his cleanliness having been established by process of law – Justice on this occasion not merely being blindfolded but having a bag over her head as well – he was aflame to get on that pole and belt the hell oot o' thae ither fowk from the ither mobs. He had, he observed, shown that — Baxter that he couldnae talk tae him like that; now, let him be provided with a pillow and give him some fighting room.

His entry being accepted, he went to bask in the glory which briefly surrounds all soldiers who have faced the ultimate military trial and got away with it. Not that there was much congratulation from his fellows; the battalion simply shook its head and remarked that he was as lucky as he was dirty. But the Bullet-headed Little Bandits, Donnie and Davie, rejoiced in his delivery, and delighted in the rumour that Corporal Baxter had wept on hearing the verdict, and had vowed to nail McAuslan for insolence in entering for the pillow-fight after all.

Saturday was clear and brilliant, and the sports field was all gay dresses and uniforms; the women were wearing the 'new look' then, with ankle-strap shoes and big, bucket hats; the sun shone on green grass and white marquees and panting Highlanders in singlets; there were refreshments and small talk and the tinkle of well-bred laughter, and in the distance the beat of pipes and drums from the little arena where the dancing and piping were being judged. Royalty was there in the person of a Duchess, surrounded by a gracefully inclining crowd from which there rose a continual hum of murmured pleasantries and nervous jealousy. There were officers of rank, blazered civilians, elderly gentlemen with kilts too long and memories even longer; young officers whose accents had grown remarkably refined overnight flirted with the Edinburgh belles; there were the occasional rumbles of applause as a race finished, and much calculating as the results came in to decide which regiment was out in front; the pipe-sergeant, skipping with nervousness, was there to hustle the adjutant, flushed from his victory in the high jump, to the dancing stage, inquiring anxiously about strains and ruptures; the various colonels affected a fine disinterest in the competitive side of things and watched the scoreboard like hawks; starters' guns cracked, debs squeaked, subalterns giggled, sergeants swore softly, hats were raised, glasses were emptied, programmes were consulted, and I weighed up the lean, sallow Cameron Highlander who had clipped two seconds off my time in the heat of the quarter, and wondered if I had an extra five yards somewhere in me for the final.

As it turned out, I hadn't. In spite of the gallant blocking tactics of Corporal Pudden, that Cameron hung at my elbow like a shadow, and in the final straight, when he drew ahead, I made my burst too soon and hadn't anything left for the last twenty yards. He could have beaten me anywhere, any time, I think, so it made no odds. A Black Watch came third.

We took the relay, however, no thanks to me, for running fourth I inherited a lead of thirty yards which a lanky Seaforth reduced to five; he came desperately near to catching me at the finish, but at the risk of thrombosis and nervous exhaustion I managed to stay in front.

We were doing respectably enough, one way and another, for the tug-of-war team were having a field day in the heats of that event, thanks to the colossal weight of the battalion cooks, under their sergeant, and the tremendous brawn of Provost Sergeant McCarry and Wee Wullie, who was the anchor. The cook-sergeant, or master gyppo, was only about five feet high, but he was about eighteen stone in weight, and his assistant cooks were full of high living and endurance. McGarry would have given a gorilla a run for its money, and Wee Wullie, the rope like a thread in his paw, was as immovable as the city hall. They pulled a wiry HLI team to pieces in the first round, and walked away with the Argylls in the second, to the great satisfaction of the pipe-sergeant.

'The Campbells iss beat,' said he. 'Glory to God and to the master gyppo, see the champion size of him. He is like Donald Dinnie for strength, or A. A. Cameron that could lift a Clydesdale horse and cart. Wait you till they meet the Black Watch in the final, and some of the Colonel's good manners will disappear; he cannae abide the Black Watch. I don't mind them mysel'; it's the Argylls I cannae stomach. I'll go over to their pipey, Sergeant Macarthur, in a minute and have a wee gloat.'

The day wore on in a golden haze; I spent most of my time lolling on a grassy bank, smoking the cigarettes which I had been avoiding while in training, strolling up to the marquee for lunch, full of content that the battalion was acquitting itself well (not that the sports officer gets any credit for that, only blame if they do badly), and stopping by the children's sports in the afternoon to watch Donnie and Davie perform in the infants' foot-race. A good proportion of the crowd were here, including the Duchess and her train; children get them every time.

Fortunately the well-bred spectators were at a sufficient distance not to see the raw work that was being pulled in some of the events. I watched a tiny blonde of the Argyll and Sutherlands take the egg-and-spoon race with her egg firmly clamped down by a thumb, and in the boys' obstacle race things happened during the crawl under the tarpaulin that would have disgraced a gladiatorial combat. One unfortunate little Seaforth emerged into the light crying, with his belt knotted round his ankles – yes, there are lessons in imperial history even in a regimental children's athletic meeting.

But the infants' foot-race was a horror. I had reassured myself by careful inquiry beforehand that the wise money was riding on Davie at odds on, with Donnie evens and no one else quoted. The thing appeared to be sewn up, and the Bullet-headed Little Bandits set a cracking pace after some excellent elbow-work at the start. They were neck and neck to within feet of the tape, and then Donnie stumbled, his brother checked instinctively, and a foxy-faced little ruffian in the Camerons shot through to take the decision literally by a head.

There was light laughter and applause from the gallery, and obscene lamentation from the defeated participants. I saw Davie's little gargoyle face distorted with grief as the stewards shooed him away, while Donnie appeared to be entering some form of official protest; he almost caught the Cameron child by the tea-tent, but fear lent the winner wings and he escaped. I reflected that it was going to take more than a mere bedtime story to console the twins for this.

I was studying the scoreboard back at the main arena when the pipe-sergeant skipped up to announce that we had come third in the piping and second in the dancing, which wass not too bad at all, at all, 'although mind you, Mr MacNeill, sir, there is chudges there that are more concerned to give the prizes to regiments wi' royal colonels-in-chief than to honest dancers. I'm no' sayin' the princess had anythin' to do wi' it, mind, but there's an HLI man yonder wi' a winner's ticket an' him wi' no more grace and music than the MO's dog. He iss chust a yokel.'

'Never mind,' I said, counting up. 'If we take a place in the pillow-fight and win the tug-of-war we'll finish top of this heap yet.' They were the only events left, and from all over the ground people were converging on the space in front of the stand where the pillow-fight tank stood below the royal box; the preliminary rounds were already being decided amidst shrieks of laughter and monumental splashings, and the pipey and I made our way round until we could get a view of the tank and the combatants crouched precariously on the pole two feet above the water's chilly surface.

The science of pillow-fighting lies in the balance. You sit astride the pole, legs dangling or crossed beneath it, and hammer your opponent with your pillow (which after the first few rounds is sopping wet and heavy). The trick is hitting with controlled force, for if you swing wildly and miss, your own momentum will put you in the drink.

McAuslan didn't know this, but he had a technique of his own, and it worked. Of course, being more ape than man he had an advantage, but no idea of how to exploit it. He just sat astride, ankles locked, hair plastered down, head sunk between his shoulders, face shining with bestial fear, and clung to the pole like a limpet. Let them hit him all they wanted, he didn't care; the word went round that he was paralysed with fear at the thought of contact with water, which may well have been true. At any event, he won two bouts against opponents who overbalanced in their energy, while McAuslan, without striking a blow, concentrated on staying perpendicular.

His third fight was a closer thing, for he was up against the Seaforth colonel's batman, a herculean thug who battered so hard that McAuslan fell sideways but managed to keep his feet wrapped round the pole, and hung head down above the water. The batman thrashed away at him, leaning over to get at him, and McAuslan in his desperation managed to catch the other's pillow and drag him down to destruction.

This feat received the biggest cheer of the day, while McAuslan, clinging on like some great sloth, worked his way along the pole to safety.

'That brute's prehensile,' muttered the Seaforth colonel, and our colonel, the very one who had seen McAuslan consigned to a court-martial, said happily that he wouldn't be surprised.

It would be nice to record that McAuslan continued to triumph through the final round, but it didn't happen. I was beginning to wonder if Corporal Baxter's well-meant efforts to introduce our contestant to water were not going to be frustrated after all, when he met his match. It was an epic contest, in its way, for McAuslan was pitted in the final against the Argyll's padre, a fat and sporting cleric, toughened by countless General Assemblies, and with a centre of gravity so low that he was practically immovable.

He swung a powerful pillow, but for once McAuslan, supposing no doubt that since his opponent was a man of God he would be a soft touch, came out swinging himself. They clobbered each other heartily for a few seconds, and then McAuslan's pillow slipped from his hand, and he was left defenceless. He gave a despairing cry, the crowd roared, and the padre, full of the lust of holy slaughter like Archbishop Turpin at Roncesvalles, humped along the pole for the kill. He brandished his pillow aloft, and McAuslan, all decency gone, grappled with him; they swayed together for a moment, and then with shrieks of shipwreck and foundered mariners, they plunged into the tank.

The surface boiled and heaved for a few moments, and then the padre emerged with a fine porpoise action, and was understood to complain that McAuslan had bitten his foot. Presently the culprit broke surface, looking like Grendel's mother, to be disqualified for wrestling and ungentlemanly conduct, or whatever it is called under pillow-fighting rules. It was fair enough, I suppose, and my sympathies were with the limping padre, Argyll though he was. Any man who has had McAuslan gnawing at him under four feet of water deserves all the commiseration he can get.

After this the tug-of-war was an anti-climax, especially as we disposed of the Black Watch in two straight pulls, despite the fact that Wee Wullie had obviously taken a liquid lunch ('weel gassed,' observed the pipe-sergeant, 'stiffer than a caber') and insisted on pulling sideways instead of straight back. This seemed to alarm the Black Watch more than his own side, who were used to him, and the massive strength of McGarry and the master-gyppo did the rest.

There remained only the prize-giving, presided over by the Duchess, with RSM Mackintosh beside her in full fig, roaring out the names as the winners came forward. If you have seen one sports prize-giving you have seen them all; the polite clapping and murmurs of 'Ahhm, well done' from the Quality gathered behind the platform, and the cries of 'Aw-haw-hey, we're a wee boys' from the hoi polloi out in front as their champions are rewarded; the little table with its silverware and certificates; the tousled competitors hurrying up to shake hands and receive their prizes; the cool Duchess (or whoever it is) in her picture hat, smiling and offering pleasant congratulations – it may happen elsewhere, but there is something uniquely British about it; it is one of those pointless important rituals that we could not conceivably give up, especially if it happens to be raining.

As battalion sports officer, I collected the shield along with my opposite number from the Camerons – when everything was tallied up it was discovered that our regiments had tied for first place – and the rest of the presentations went more or less according to plan: Wee Wullie did not fall down when he and the tug-of-war specialists came forward; the pipe-sergeant, I was intrigued to notice, for all his strictures on the winner of the dancing, cheered and applauded wildly when that worthy received his trophy. But what fascinated me most was to see McAuslan shamble up behind the Argyll padre to receive his runners-up award for the pillow-fight: someone should have photographed it – McAuslan getting a prize for something.

Being him, he hadn't had time to change, and only last-minute modesty had caused him to put on his tunic above his sodden gym shorts; he was, as usual, in a state of acute anxiety, and he shook hands with the Duchess like a badly wound-up clockwork toy, clutching his prize of saving certificates as if it was a reprieve.

She smiled at him as he stood dripping and shuffling, and then – I'm prepared to believe that royalty are clairvoyant – to the statutory 'Well done' she added:

'You must be dreadfully chilly; I'm sure you'll be glad to get into your nice uniform again.'

It was kindly meant, of course, and it was certainly kindly received. Probably only the RSM and I appreciated the full irony of it, but McAuslan blossomed like a June flower. As if a court-martial wasn't enough, here was a Duchess implying that he, McAuslan, wasnae dirty; for a moment he looked like Galahad receiving the victor's crown from a Queen of Beauty, and it wouldn't have astonished me if he had knelt and pressed the hem of her dress to his lips. But he did the Glasgow equivalent, which was to blush and say, 'Och, ta, but,' and then withdrew, trailing damp clouds of glory.

No doubt there was a moral in it somewhere; McAuslan, the dirtiest soldier in the world, getting prizes and escaping unscathed from courts-martial and having Duchesses paying him indirect compliments: considering, I decided that the kindly providence that watches over drunks and children must be guiding McAuslan's destiny as well. I just hoped it wouldn't work too hard; the kind of luck he'd been having he'd probably end up Chief of the Imperial General Staff. Mind you, we've had nearly as bad.

And that was it, apart from one trivial incident which shortened a few life expectancies and, to me at least, was a fitting epilogue to a fairly eventful few days. The children received their prizes right at the finish, and one of the last was the award to the winner and runner-up of the infants' eighty-yard dash. The Quality were smiling indulgently as the little dears came forward, the Duchess was at her most charming, the crowd applauded loudly, and even RSM Mackintosh wore a paternal expression.

And then little Donnie stepped forward to receive his second prize. The Duchess beamed on him fondly – in his little kilt, and with his normal lowering expression, he looked like a rather cute little Highland bull – shook his hand, and said:

'I think you ran very well; and you were really unlucky not to win.'

To which the gentle child, lifting up his earnest gargoyle face, replied in the accent of Maryhill Road, but with fearful clarity:

'Ach, yon Cameron — tripped me. It was — swiz.'

There was a few seconds' horrified frozen silence, in which the Duchess' charming smile altered by not one fraction, and a ghastly sigh rippled through the ranks of the Quality. And then RSM Mackintosh, his years of Guards' training no doubt coming to his aid, leaned forward and said in a diplomatic whisper which was audible twenty yards away:

'He is saying "Thank you very much", your highness. In Gaelic.'

You cannot shake a Regimental Sergeant-Major; whatever the situation, he is unconquerable.

'How very nice of him,' said the Duchess, still smiling, as Donnie trotted away. 'How awfully nice.'

You cannot shake a royal Duchess either.

RUSSELL THORNDIKE

DR. SYN

ON THE HIGH SEAS

**THE SCHOLARLY PARSON AND THE DREADED PIRATE—
AND ONLY ONE MAN KNEW THEY WERE THE SAME!**

"I am a dead man—and no one will know."

That morning the young Vicar of Dymchurch had been a happy man—happy in his work and his marriage. Then a letter from his wife had blasted his life . . . burned out the scholar and gentleman, leaving only a demonic figure driven by a passion for revenge. And Syn's quest for vengeance took him to the far parts of the world, to scenes of high adventure and battle—and to the depths of his own personal Hell.

DR. SYN

is one of the great creations of adventurous fiction—the benevolent parson the world knows, the daring outlaw his underworld associates see.

$ .95

To order by mail, send 95¢ per book plus 25¢ per order for handling to Ballantine Cash Sales, P.O. Box 505, Westminster, Maryland 21157. Please allow three weeks for delivery.

FICTION
from

BALLANTINE BOOKS